reINcarnate

By

Patrick Querney

reINcarnate

Patrick Querney

PART ONE

CHAPTER ONE

When Cil Franklin opened his eyes, he knew it was for the last time. He laid on his bed wet with water dripping from his ceiling that hadn't been fixed for decades, but this didn't bother him. His family never understood him or his dream, nor had they bothered to talk to him for years — he didn't receive even one Christmas card. The only damn thing that bothered him was the kid upstairs, playing *Guitar Hero* 15 hours a day. Oh, yes – that annoyed him immensely.

I'm not going out when that stupid Foghat song is being played — which lead him to pick up the phone.

"Hello?" The old lady's voice penetrated his ch'i.

"Ms. Garnand, it's Cil from room 112." He was getting groggy from the pills and had to fight to keep his thoughts coherent. "Can I speak to little Davie?"

"Uh, yea. What about?" coughing as the cigarettes took their toll on her voice.

"It's about that game he plays." his voice becoming groggier.

"Ok." She yelled, "Davie!"

"Hello?" The boy's clean voice came through.

"Hey Davie, you fucking suck at guitar" — he hung up

the phone.

A brief silence followed as the storm approached with a loud yell — a door slammed. Hammering the door, he let her pound. He was close, so close and the sound of pounding faded away.

CHAPTER TWO

Cil knew from a long time what lay beyond: he had died once and saw a bright light. He didn't buy it when everyone told him it was the light from the operating room. Since then, he threw himself into the writings from a strange British guy who submerged himself into the occult, Aleister Crowley. This is when his family stopped communicating with him.

Cil didn't share the same enthusiasm as Crowley's love for drugs and orgies. He figured that this made him cleaner and more aware. Life was energy: when death came and took the fragile shell, the energy had to go somewhere. Death was never an end, but energy is forever.

It could be managed or transferred. Maybe he could live again when his body engaged in a slow roar. The heart was only a muscle: it's strange that it was the first to develop and the last to end it all. He was only a 3-week-old when his heart became and a 57-year-old when it stopped. He often mused in the cycle of life, but there was more — he spent the last 23 years delving into that.

The stroke was the starter, then he lost the use of his right hand. He had to learn to wipe his ass using his left. In the beginning, it was something that resulted in a lot of messy situations, however, he got his right hand back.

***

Breaking from the past, Cil found himself laying on the bed with his feces staining the already stained sheets. He knew he was leaving on a strange trip and getting up to use the bathroom didn't make much sense. If it did work — well! Whoever found his dead body would not be happy. He closed his eyes: the ribbons of multi-colored beams of movement cut through the darkness. His heart slowed and squeezed out a couple of more squirts of blood — then it stopped.

What came next was something no one could talk about: a wisp of something cold sneaked out from the still body. At first, it was just a stream but gradually, it grew bigger: like a crappy car engine spitting out a huge glob of smog. But this was almost yellow — neither it had an odor nor form. This apparition found an open window and slipped out into the wet world. It hovered for a short time and moved toward the rusty stairwell until it meandered down to the dirty alley. It snuck around boxes, trash cans, and the grease trap from the Chinese restaurant. The back door was open: the sound of clatter and conversations blended with the rain. The yellow formless apparition didn't go in though it paused like it wanted to — suddenly, another sound pinched the din of the everyday world.

"Meow!"

It was a scraggly cat about to rummage through the garbage. It could have been a handsome cat, if it wasn't so dirty. The substance was still, Cil backed away, but the cat was as curious as its reputation. The semi-conscious nature of the energy, soul, or whatever you want to call it blinked for a second and disappeared — the cat had it.

***

In the dementia filled void, the in-between state of the man's segues wrapped itself into the feline: human thoughts filled its brain.

Mother fucker! I'm in a damn cat.

The experiment worked, but the outcome was not what Cil wanted. Well, "wanted" was a stretch, as Cil had no idea what would happen. It was amazing that it worked in the first place. Now, he would have to live as a cat for a while until he figured out how to switch to something more desirable — if he figured out.

Being in a cat puts the kibosh on things. The plan, no matter how thinly it was formulated, was that Cil would sneak into a man's body. His essence would replace that of the host and he would become the world's most prolific serial killer. All the blame would go to the host, and then to the next one and so on. Thinking this whole thing through kind of got him settled on the backburner. The excitement of doing it replaced all the logical thoughts. Cil wasn't a smart man — he figured he'd just whip from man to man until he grew tired of the game which he begun.

Cil Franklin wanted to kill all his life, but he never had the guts to actually do it. When he started reading about the occult and other satanic rituals, he believed he might be able to reincarnate himself. If he could do that, he could kill without limits and get away with it. The world wouldn't get to know him as Cil Franklin, but as the crimes of Frank Smith, John Doe, or Susan, the fat prostitute.

Cil, the cat, now had some things to do: it surprised him that his intellect, thought loosely used, was intact. A cat thinking like a man! Now, that was something new. *I can still kill: I can kill cats, birds, rats and...* Ah! it all began to work out.

So Cil, the cat, continued with its original plan of eating leftover Chinese food. It had to fatten itself up to be a force to reckon with. Might as well get some fucking out of the way which Cil, the man, didn't do much.

For the next two nights, Cil, the cat, tore through the patch of land surrounding the Chinese restaurant. He had only one kill to his credit. Pickings were easy for a well-fed cat in these parts. Once, on a late night, he ran across a not so well fed female and had a loud session of kitty sex — he killed the poor thing, Praying Mantis style. He didn't eat it though, but the thought did cross his mind.

During the day, when cats slept, he would try to forge a plan to get on to do something bigger. Being a cat in the city wasn't easy — he almost got flattened by a car. He didn't want to run across any dogs, unless he was one. Being killed prematurely might end his cycle, and as he figured: it was he who had to die on his own terms to move on. As a man, he spoke the jibber-jabber that made the passing possible. It took him years to master the right incantation. He assumed he had it right one morning, as he lay on his crap stained bed, when he was able to leave his body and look at the wretched thing from a few feet above. Now, he would have to think of the spell — "Meow" he figured, wouldn't do the trick.

***

On the evening of his fifth night, he wandered across a stray dog. It was sleeping, but when he crept close: it opened its eyes and looked into his. Some semblance of cat instinct reared up in him, and his tail shot straight up and hissed. He didn't want to hiss, but a cat was a cat — even though this cat was a little more. The dog didn't mind, and watched him lazily. A weird thought slipped into Cil's head: a caring thought. As a young boy, Cil loved animals — he didn't care much for people, but animals were different. Hurting them wasn't his manner. Hence, regret for killing that cat appeared: it had been way back in his subconscious, but now it surfaced.

I don't want to hurt this thing.

Empathy moved him — it had been covered for long. For a cat brain weighed only ounces, but for a human it's pounds. The decision to leave the dog alone was finalized — he moved on.

***

The plan temporally changed when Cil went about strategizing on how to get into a man. He didn't know how old the cat was and the idea of getting himself into the pound entered his brain. But what if he wasn't adopted? What would happen if he was being put down? This wouldn't work — it's harder than he thought.

Wait a minute. I'm a scumbag, but not all people are scumbags, so if I hang around houses for a while, maybe someone will bring me in.

This is great — why didn't he think of that sooner? Screw hanging around garbage: some people were nice and kids loved cats. There were apartments nearby and he made his way to them.

Queens, New York was a decent place: it was the largest of the five boroughs and Manhattan wasn't far away. Mostly, middle-class folks lived here. Long Island City, where he was now, was crowded but livable. Cil's apartment, which was stinking pretty badly by now, from his week-old dead body, was almost on the water. It was on 21st street and he could walk, even as a cat, over the Queensboro Bridge to Roosevelt Island. He had done it many times as a man, visited the old, smallpox hospital that lay in ruins. There was a school and he would wait upon the children as they ventured out to play, watching them — he tried to remember what it was like being young.

The East River divided him from Manhattan and that itself was foul: probably due to the bodies that rest in the deep. If he couldn't find a host where he was, he would venture over there. He thought to stop by his apartment, to take a look at his old human body, but it went up in vapor as soon as it manifested. That was old news — better to leave the crappy past behind.

* * *

Over the past few years, many Latino folks moved into his neighborhood and fat little Mexican kids ran around the blocks taking up other people's time. He didn't have anything against Mexicans, but being one didn't float his boat: so, going over to Manhattan seemed the best choice. New York drivers didn't care much for each other, nonetheless cats, so he was careful while crossing the bridge. There were quite a few people walking and he meandered his way around until he reached Roosevelt Island. There was a nursing home next to the hospital, on the Northern end of the island, and he made his way there. It was almost sunset and many elderly people wandered around. Some looked lost, but dementia is a strange thing. Growing old was terrible, but being put away by your own family made the matter worse. Sadly, in most nursing homes the lost and forgotten occupied its rooms. People stashed away by people who had no time for them. Sick! Humans! What a disgusting race.

* * *

By the time the sun set, most of the old folks hobbled and wheeled their way back into the faded-building — Cil was alone once more. As dusk approached, amplified noises stretched out from everywhere. When the lights were no more, Cil became aware that he was not the only cat. At first, he tried to stand his ground, but this was not his territory: the seasoned cats were bastards. Once he tried to hide away near the dumpster, behind the hospital, he was charged by a pack of angry locals. He sprinted almost a quarter of the way across the island before he realized the pack had long stopped the chase. Cats were amazing: they would scare away strangers, then leave them be.

Cil was still filled up with his yesterday's meal. So, he found a dry place, on top of a shed, and there he kept watch for the night. There was always another morning, but the night was not without excitement. He swatted a few cats from his perch: whether they wanted to mate or beat him he did not know, but he had the high ground and it did him well. He marked the edges of the shed and planned the next day's adventures.

The earth rolled until the sun sneaked over the east coast, drying up puddles of rain water. And like an alarm, it drove the elderly out of their prisons — like an army. Children with funny backpacks swarmed around, getting ready for a full day of boredom. There were Transformers, Batman, Dora the Explorer, and many regular Walmart backpacks. It's interesting how kids and old people, who are at opposite ends of the spectrum of life, meet.

As a cat, Cil liked morning — unlike most cats, who were sleeping, he didn't have to run all over the island to escape a nasty death. He sat along the water's edge, on the east side of the island, watching people come and go. And about mid-day, he saw an elderly, black woman wheel her way along the street. She didn't ask for money or food, but only sought companionship.

Cil approached her — "Why, hello there, little fella." She reached down and petted him: it felt like out of this world. A strange rumbling bubbled within: he didn't understand it, as first, but realized — *I'm purring*! What a cool sensation it was. His whole body felt electric and other pressing concerns washed away. He laid down and offered his tummy, the elderly lady rubbed him until he set aside all thoughts of becoming anything else. If there was a Heaven, which Cil didn't believe in, this was what it felt like — but she stopped and went away.

The sun made him lazy and all he wanted to do was sleep, but it would have to wait. He explored a little and saw an elderly man feeding the ducks, except there were no ducks. The man was mumbling something which Cil couldn't understand. He figured the man was little nuts which was a perfect fit. Cil crept closer but the man didn't notice him. He was deeply concentrating on spreading breadcrumbs to his imaginary friends.

"Meow!"

Nothing.

"Meow! Meow!"

"What the fuck do you want? You're scaring away the birds. Get the hell out of here," said the elderly man.

Cil didn't give up: he rubbed against the man's legs and let his purring be heard which he learned to control.

"All right, come on up. The ducks don't like me anyway." The old man patted his right thigh and motioned the cat to jump up, which it did. More rubbing and purring: soon, both were in a sublime state of general euphoria — it was time.

CHAPTER THREE

The transformation was sudden as Cil's essence floated into the old man's mouth. The brittle body still hurt, but a much younger man was inside. His senses changed from acute to dim, but he was a human again. Deep inside, the old man struggled for only a second, then gave up. Maybe he realized it was for the better, but those thoughts faded away. The cat, now just another stray, snapped and jumped off Cil's lap, confused as to why he was there. Before the thing went out of sight, it looked back and leaped.

Cil stood up and searched for memories about the room number, but he couldn't find — it was a Tabula Rasa. It didn't matter anyway; he was old and could ask someone inside. The old body creaked as he moved, but it felt great to walk on two legs again.

Cil walked a couple hundred feet or so to the front door: they didn't have automatic doors in the nursing home. At the front desk, a fat woman with a lousy disposition looked up without any sign of recognition. She was shoveling a black donut into her mouth.

"What can I do for you?" She asked without emotion.

"I forgot my room number," Cil responded.

"Name?"

A piece of donut landed on the fake marble desk in front of her.

"Uh, I…"

"You don't know your name?"

"No."

The fat lady mumbled something about damn old people and wiped her mouth with her arm.

"Let me see your wrist."

When he hesitated, not knowing why she wanted to see that, she stood up and grabbed his left arm to see the blue band on his wrist.

"Grant Mooser."

She read and sat back — the thud of her large behind punishing the poor chair. She tapped the computer keyboard for a few seconds.

"405! Your room is 405."

"How do I get there?" Cil asked.

The fat woman looked at him like he was the most pathetic thing on the planet. Cil felt the anger rise in him as he glared at her.

"You go up the elevator."

She pointed to her right.

"Then you get out of the elevator and walk down the hall till you reach the room 405. After that, you put your key into the keyhole and turn it until the door unlocks then you go in. Stay inside as long as you want. There's a place called a bathroom with a thing called a toilet, which you use to go pee and poo, but from the smell of you it seems that you've already taken care of that."

Cil was really getting pissed.

"You're not very nice," he said.

"Room 405."

She repeated, waving him off like a mosquito.

Cil lingered for a moment and then began walking toward the elevator. He pushed the button and waited. When the doors opened, he stuck his foot in to stop them from closing and called back.

"When is your shift over?" he asked.

"10:00 pm," she called back without looking up.

Cil, in his old man's body, stepped into the elevator with a smile.

***

The room was pretty sparse: whatever family the old man had, if he had any, didn't supply him much. There was a single bed with a line attached to an emergency call switch. The room had a dresser with three drawers and an old 19-inch TV on a chipped away stand in the corner. He checked out the bathroom, which also had an emergency call switch — this would do for the time being.

Cil sat on the edge of the bed with one thing on his mind: he badly wanted to take care of that witch. He discovered he wore a watch, on his right wrist, and was happy to see it was close to 7:00 pm.

Three hours, baby. I'll see you in three hours.

He sat there — barely moving: and as the time hit 9:45 pm, he left his room and climbed down the stairs leading to the back of the building. Directly in front of him was a parking lot, he noticed two Mercedes-Benzes and figured it was for the staff. Just after 10:00 pm, the fat lady walked around the building toward a batch of cars — Cil made a move.

He was slow and old, but she was fat, so neither of them was going to win any race. When he got within ten feet of her, she spun around and gave him the same pathetic look that she blessed him with earlier.

"What are you doing out here? It's past curfew. Ah! You probably don't even remember that, do you?"

He walked closer

"I just wanted to thank you for helping me today," he

said.

He was now within arm's reach.

"Sure, now go back to your room or I'll call security."

"We have security?" asked Cil taking one step closer.

"All right! You senile old bastard."

She reached into her purse to get her cell phone and that's when Cil lunged at her. He was weak, but motivation does amazing things — he managed to get behind her. She was a large woman and getting his arms around her wasn't an easy task. He wrapped his right arm around her neck and squeezed with all his strength. She struggled and Cil had to lean back to win the balance.

Cil was breathing hard and was rapidly running out of power. Thinking that the car was behind him, he fell backwards, but found only an empty space. He landed on his back and it knocked the air out of him. He temporarily lost his hold, and the nurse kicked and tried to roll over, but Cil snaked his arm over her neck and locked in the chokehold. The nurse was too tired to fight anymore and the last ten-to-twelve seconds were easy. He held on almost a minute more before he released his whale. His right arm limply fell to the side and he lay there, on the concrete parking lot, chest heaving and breaths coming out like smoke from an old dying car. It took almost five minutes for him to gather strength and to move on.

CHAPTER FOUR

His first human kill exhilarated him deeply — his adrenaline rushed like a fuel injector. As he sat on his bed, shaking, he inched his body down completely, letting the wave run its course as he fell asleep. His eyes opened after fourteen hours: a short spurt of fear erupted before he realized where he was. The ceiling was different from the one he spent looking at most of his adult life. It caused a temporary shock, but the memory sank in as usual — he smiled.

The noise of shuffling feet and squeaky wheels, from outside, snapped him from his glee compelling him to walk toward the door. As he opened a little, an army of old geezers flooded down the hall. As the saying goes: when you are in Rome, do as Romans do — thus, Cil left his apartment to join the herd. It took three elevator trips to get all the folks down, as some took the stairs; when he arrived, the smell of potatoes filled the air.

It must be lunch time, he followed everyone to the dining room. The atmosphere was strange, filled with a tizzy; a group of old folks and nurses congregated near the piano. He wondered if they suspected, but no one looked at him. People sat at their designated places. Most of the people didn't mind the level of stress filling the room, while some didn't know where they were — technically, it didn't mean anything.

Cil walked toward the piano.

"… believe it or not, Nurse Becker is dead! Strangled, they say. The police have been here all morning."

Cil joined and listened for a few minutes.

"Her body was found next to her car. Someone killed her last night after her shift."

Cil entered the conversation.

"Which one was Nurse Becker?"

"She was the mean bitch who worked the swing shift," said a man around 70.

He had his haircut high and tight, Cil wondered if he was an ex-marine.

Someone else chimed in.

"Yea, Nurse Becker was the fat one. Must've been a strong son of a gun who killed her — she looked strong."

Not strong enough, he heard what he wanted and went about trying to find his table; he was starving.

***

Each table had 4 chairs — toward the middle of the room, he saw one with an empty seat, so he took it.

"This is not your table. You sit over there."

A man pointed toward a seat located next to the window.

"Does it matter?" Cil asked.

He laughed inside about these old people's picky nature.

"It matters to me! Norma sits here: we fucked last night, so she stays here. When I start fucking you, you can sit here."

Cil didn't know who Norma was, but the thought of this guy having sex was funny — he laughed.

The man took it well.

"Yea. Now! Who are you fucking?"

Cil grinned, got up and went to his table. Lunch wasn't so bad: it consisted of Salisbury steak, mashed potatoes with overdone wrinkled peas.

After lunch, most of the people went back to their rooms. A few stayed behind to watch the TV in the common area. There was a Clint Eastwood western on and Cil thought about staying, but he had things to do. He went back to his room and sat by the window planning his next adventure. It was difficult; he didn't know or hate anyone enough to kill. But he had time — there was a roof above his head, a bed with 3 meals per day; it beats being a cat.

As next morning arrived: mild tension about Nurse Becker's death subsided since nobody really cared. Most of the staff hated her, so she wasn't missed. The police didn't have any leads; it became just another cold case sitting in the silver filing cabinet at Precinct 43.

In the following week, Cil tried to meet many people as possible. He went to every meal and walked around Roosevelt Island many times. One of the things he enjoyed the most was sitting by the water, watching life move along; there were tugboats, trash barges, and an occasionally Coast Guard Cutter. Even after a week, he didn't find anyone to hate. Old people were their own manifestos: they did what they did and that's it. You can't blame someone for not knowing something because time treated them badly — growing old was hard enough.

***

The New York subway ran almost everywhere and the five boroughs were his oyster. It was a Tuesday when Cil finally got on the subway. At first, he thought to travel to Manhattan, the idea of lingering around Central Park was enticing, but the old body couldn't manage to walk that distance. He would have to navigate around the park, so, he narrowed his trip to Brooklyn. There was only a half mile to the subway which he used to travel to Linden Boulevard. He didn't know the area, but that was what he wanted - to be foreign in a foreign land. He found out that he was in Flatbush. He walked for a while and passed a hospital. It was much bigger than the one he was living in. The adventure of being in a strange place excited him. That made it easy to put his pain away. He continued walking till he reached Prospect Park, where he found a bench and rested for over an hour. Next to the park was a zoo in which people were milling in their usual New York style with really no place to go.

The park had a Botanical Garden and the Brooklyn Museum. Also, a college located toward the east — it was a good spot and he waited. Dawn approached, the sky turned from mild yellow to a shady blue and he still sat on the old bench. On the bench, the name Rebecca Fields was engraved: he wondered briefly who she was and if she was dead. When night came and the darkness half settled, the ebb of people slowed and only a few mingled. Above him hung a lamp attracting insects which swarmed around thinking it was the sun. He let himself get lost in the darkness as the low hum comforted him.

He was still in his night trance when two gay men walked by holding hands. They looked at him without much concern and continued on their way. Twenty minutes passed before anyone came by: this time it was a young punk with his pants hanging halfway down his ass. The kid, maybe 18 or 19, eyeballed him as he walked by, but after a few minutes, the kid paused and turned around heading toward Cil with a smile on his face.

"Wach ya doin', old man?"

Cil didn't answer.

"You deaf?"

"I can hear fine, son. What do you want?" Cil responded.

The kid crept closer.

"It's not safe here for geezers, ya know."

"I'm not worried about it. Are you planning on robbing me?"

"That would be too easy. I could if I wanted to."

"You wouldn't get much," said Cil and winked at him.

The wink surprised the kid — his face contorted to something like amazement.

"You a homo?" he asked.

"Listen punk! You're messing up my quiet time: if you want to rob me — rob me. If not, push off."

Cil leaned back against the hard bench and folded his arms across his chest, then an idea popped up.

"Unless you want something else?"

"Yea, old man. I want you to suck my dick. It'll save me the time on kicking your ass."

That was what Cil was hoping for, his idea was turning into a plan and it was working nicely.

"Ok kid, let's see what you have got."

The kid laughed a little, which changed into a grin as he unzipped his pants — the night got deeper. The punk was proud of what he was packing and once the equipment was out, Cil slid off the bench and on to his knees — he went to work.

Thoughts bounced between the two hemispheres of his brain dulling the act he was doing. *Once I'm out of this body, it won't matter. I won't be the one sucking a dick, I'll be the one who had his dick sucked.* It was a funny paradox since he did the act.

About a minute passed, the kid was mumbling some filthy shit by grabbing the back of Cil's head and grinding it against his penis. Cil went to work on the incantations in his head, he did them slowly and carefully. The transformation was quicker this time, he looked down at the confused old man and pushed his head away. The old man fell back against the bench. He looked wildly at the young kid. Cil zipped up his business and walked away, and after a few feet, he stopped and pulled up his pants realizing that he looked like an idiot — he didn't look back.

***

The clothes Cil wore didn't suit him, he went about trying to figure out a way to get new ones. He didn't know what gangs were in this area and didn't want to run into any. Walking around Brooklyn looking like a gangbanger wasn't the safest thing to do. He felt in his new pockets and found a wallet in the right back one. There were seventeen dollars, a driver's license, a few pictures of a pretty Mexican girl, and a condom.

People still put rubbers in their wallets? — he threw that away. The name on the license was Gregory Lines. He was eighteen and would turn nineteen on June 14th, which was a couple of months away. He didn't know where to go from now; the old man would go back to his home and Cil would have to find a new one himself. Cil found a cell phone in the kid's front pocket and dialed 911 to let them know an old man was in the park looking very confused — he owed the guy that much.

There was a college nearby and Cil went on his way. It was early morning and he knew he wouldn't find many students wandering — he wanted to get the lay of the land. Being young made a huge difference, and in under fifteen minutes he was there. He walked along Empire Boulevard toward the intersection of Nostrand Avenue, the buildings became visible in the night.

The building constructed with brick and glass consisted of three floors. He walked to the front and read — Medgar Evers College, written in white letters. There was an insignia that looked like a peace symbol under the lettering, it had three pictures: a scale, a lantern, and two hands making some kind of gesture which he thought was pretty neat. He walked to the east side and came upon a large glass structure that annexed the college building. He looked at the time on his new cell phone, it read 3:07 AM. It was very quiet, which was peculiar for Brooklyn. A light came on in the third floor and he slipped behind a tree, but it was just the cleaning crew.

With nothing else to do, he headed back to the park. Sleep was on his mind; he walked the mile or so, found a nice cubby spot behind the zoo, and fell asleep. Early morning rolled by; the sun snuck up radiating warm light that shook him from a deep dream. He stayed there for almost half the day, thinking about what to do next. This was a new and unexplored territory; he was a free bird and could do anything he wanted and that excited him, yet it made him nervous. What does a man do when he has nothing to do? — find his next victim.

***

At noon, he made his way back to college. As he neared, the hustle and bustle of students going back and forth to class created an energy that gave him a hard-on. He walked to the main building with the intention of going in, but realized he was the only white kid around. He stood there, twenty feet or so from the front door, and watched for a while; it became apparent that this was a black school. Now, Cil didn't care what color people were. He lived long enough to care little about people — he hated them all. He always considered himself a *Dirty Harry* kind of guy. He loved those movies. There was a part in the first or the second one where the police commissioner or someone else was talking to Harry's new partner and told him, "Harry hates everyone." The character went on with all the slang words associated with the racial slurs for all types of people: White, Black, Asian, and so on — it fit his bill.

Standing there looking like a fool made him look like, well, a fool — he went through the front doors. At first, he forgot he was in the kid's body and thought he would look out of place: then he remembered, *Play the part*, and walked toward the registration desk.

After an hour of asking questions, he exited the building and went back to the park. It was mostly a black college, but there were few white students and young ones from south of the border.

It was a clear Friday night; he walked the short distance to the college happily whistling a tune. It was 7:04 pm and students were milling about. He figured there would be a party somewhere — hell, it was Friday after all. He walked around the campus looking like he knew what he was doing and at 8:43 pm, he spotted his prey. It reminded him of a wildlife program where the lioness would wait in the brush analyzing which ibex she would target.

He had to be careful when selecting someone who couldn't overpower him. This body he inhabited was scrawny, weak, and couldn't do much. The young man he eyed was somewhere in the vicinity of one hundred and sixty pounds. Cil walked up to the man and asked him what time it was.

"Sorry man, I don't know. I don't wear a watch," said the kid.

Cil stood there looking at him, the student became nervous. Cil did look like a punk. The student walked away and Cil lost his chance, but he followed.

"Are you following me?" the kid asked.

Cil looked at him square in the eyes and smiled.

"Uh, do you have a smoke?" Cil inched closer.

"Get a job, dude."

The student walked around the high glass building to the right of the main building and picked up his pace. Cil ran up to him and pulled out the knife he found in the park. When he got closer, he plunged the blade into the kid with all the with all the force he could muster — the boy fell backwards. He reached out to study the boy; the knife ate through the flesh smoothly, and blood drained forward, like a waterfall.

The kid looked at him with a frightened wonder only fear could provide. Cil's excitement almost overloaded his senses — he felt faintish, for only a second or two. The boy's body fell backwards after Cil released his grip, it landed on the fresh grass with a muted *thump*.

The dim red light from the security post illuminated the blood, making it look crimson. Cil dragged the body into a patch of trees and finished what he started. He sawed away the hands and feet, and put them in a plastic bag: he left the body to be preyed on. Over an hour later, he was in the park where he sat on the same bench with the bag containing the parts between his legs. He smoked a cigarette and let the euphoria take him.

Sleep wanted him badly, but there was work to be done. He stood up and walked toward the zoo, where he left the right hand by the front gates. He then went to the western edge and placed the left foot near a light pole. On the southern edge, he left the right foot and carried the left hand to the Botanical Garden at the eastern end. He thought it was clever leaving the four pieces of the body in the four compass points. Long ago, he read somewhere that the word "news" was an acronym for north, east, west, and south — this would most certainly be news.

When that was done, he walked slowly back to his cubby spot and went over the day's doings. A delicate rain came and washed the blood from his hands. He took off his clothes and got them as clean as he could. As the night was a witness, he slept wearing his underwear.

CHAPTER FIVE

Pillow shaped clouds scattered the sky while the sun shyly hid behind them. Cil woke up with his back hurting; he was tired of sleeping in the park, and needed a place to call home. It was time for new body. When he exited the bushes, he saw officers prowling around talking to people — Cil became nervous — he needed to get the hell out of here as soon as possible.

A part of him wanted to see how things were going, but the forensic team were all over the place; he didn't want to push his luck further. He headed north, shooting looks over his shoulder to see if anyone was following. By now, he figured where to go from here. He lived most of his life in squalor and wanted to see it the grass was greener somewhere else. Manhattan, for sure, didn't have much grass in the city, but it was way better.

He approached the subway and got on a train. An hour later, he got off and headed west a tad to Central Park, where he would center his thoughts and plan his next move. It was a long day and the thought of sleeping in the park disturbed him. He knew better than that. If he didn't find a new body, he would have no choice. After paying for the subway, he had fifteen dollars and some change left which he could use for food — Manhattan wasn't cheap.

Dark clouds moved along slowly in contrast to the hustle and bustle representing the life in New York City. People presenting different cultures, races, and occupations, across the globe, flooded the park during lunch. Hotdog vendors and other miscellaneous food carts spread out in all directions — it was a lovely day.

***

Identifying the right target was touchy; it's vital to have a lot of information, such as who would be rich? Who would have a car? Who would have a nice apartment? Killing was the easy part, but finding out who to kill was — well! A little more complicated.

Cil watched a horse go by, tied to it was a carriage that didn't look comfortable. Its handler walked beside trying to drum up some business. Riding in a horse carriage around Central Park was exquisite, if you could afford it. The big brown animal looked sad. Cil knew what imprisonment felt like, even if it was self-imposed — he pitied the thing.

It's easy to let one's thoughts go astray while watching people. Cil almost let a gem go, but it didn't matter since that gem came and sat next to him.

"How's it going?" Cil asked.

The man wore a very nice suit – definitely Italian. The fabric was soft and shiny — it was perfectly fitting.

"Fine," replied the man.

He pulled out his cell phone and began texting. His fingers moved over the keyboard effortlessly.

"Looks like it's about to rain," Cil said.

All that man heard was "rain." He shot Cil a perturbed look and went back to his texting. *Why the hell did he look at me like that?* Then he remembered what he looked like.

"Hey! I'm not a punk kid," Cil said.

"Huh?"

"That horse just took a shit."

"Uh huh."

"I want to eat your pussy."

"Sure!"

Cil laughed — this dude didn't hear anything - perfect! When the man was done texting, he pulled out a cigar and lit it with a match. Cil pulled out a cigarette and asked for a light which the man gave, and sat back — puffing away.

"Man! Arthur Andersen, from Enron, sure screwed a lot of people, eh?" Cil said between drags.

This caught the man's attention.

"How did you know about that?"

"My father works on Wall Street. He tells me a lot. I'm trying to get into the X-Games. I'm a skateboarder."

Cil looked at the guy's eyes to see if anything was resonating.

"What does your father do?"

Smoke filled the area where they sat. A woman who walked by gave them a dirty look.

"He trades. Makes a bunch of money too. He always bitches about the way I dress, but this is who I am," lied Cil.

"Yup, money's good."

"You must have a fat apartment here in the city," Cil nudged further.

The man smiled, "How would you guess that?"

"That suit ain't cheap, dude."

Cil picked up a lot of the "youth" vernacular from watching a lot of tween shows on TV.

"No son, cheap it was not. Don't they have a skate park here?" The man asked.

"Yea, but I'm bored with it. Too many wannabees there."

Cil was getting tired of the banter and wanted to cut it off well.

"Well, it was nice talking to you. I've got to get home."

"You too. Take care."

Cil got up and walked a short distance away. He figured

the man would eventually leave, so Cil stationed himself directly across from where the man was sitting and waited.

After thirty minutes, the man headed toward Fifth Avenue and Cil followed — at a distance, of course. The man's cigar was only halfway done, he worked on the rest of it as he walked. The smoke drifted backwards and Cil breathed it in. It wasn't long until the man turned right and headed for an immaculate building. A doorman opened the door and the man walked through thanking the old fellow with a clap on the shoulder.

Cil was in a predicament: there was no way that doorman would let him in. He stood outside, trying to hatch a plan. An idea popped up; he pulled out the kid's wallet.

"Excuse me, sir.

That man who just went in dropped his wallet, and I want to give it back."

"You mean Mr. Cafferty?" The doorman asked.

"Yea, he works with my father. I know I don't look like it, but my father works on Wall Street. I was talking to Mr. Cafferty in the park, and he offered me a cigar, but I don't smoke — my dad says it will kill ya."

"Ok, give it to me and I'll see to it."

The old doorman held out his gloved hand.

"I'd rather give it to him myself. My father would beat my butt if I didn't do the right thing. I know his apartment — we've been there before. Last time, I got punished by my father for sampling some of Mr. Cafferty's wine."

The doorman looked at Cil for a second, then nodded his head.

"All right. Go on in."

Cil figured the doorman has just seen everything before, and he was surprised that his ruse worked. The wallet he showed the old man was tattered and was not the billfold a rich dude would have, but it worked. He walked down the beautiful hallway decorated with paintings on both sides and a plush eastern style carpet. A mailbox was on the right and

Cil found Mr. Cafferty's apartment number on that — 504.

Cil walked to the elevator and pushed "5" and rode up. When the door opened, a well-dressed lady came in as Cil left — she smelled great. *Living the good life would suit him*, it was about time. He walked down the corridor and stopped at the apartment. He took a deep breath and knocked.

***

The sound of the door being unlocked broke Cil from his nervousness — the door opened. Cafferty was in a towel — he was in amazing shape, well-formed muscles and muscular arms. He gave Cil a once-over and recognized him from the park.

"What are you doing here?" The man asked.

Cil didn't have an answer, so he punched the guy and pushed him back. There was a lamp on an antique table, Cil grabbed and crashed it over the man's head knocking him down. Cil quickly shut the door and punched him out unconscious. He was out of breath, but he surveyed the apartment; it was nice — very nice. The living room was decorated in minimalism style, with a few expensive paintings on the walls. A wine rack took up most of the eastern wall: Cil got up and picked a bottle from the rack. He didn't know Shinola about wine and sure as hell didn't know he picked an expensive one. He walked to the kitchen and opened the drawers until he found the corkscrew, which he used sloppily to open the bottle. He took a long swig and set it down on the counter which was made of real marble. He ran his fingers along the top; he never felt anything like this.

The rest of the apartment was equally nice. The bedroom had a king size bed with five hundred thread count sheets, a sixty-five-inch flat screen TV, and an Onkyo stereo system gracing an elaborate shelving unit. He took a trip into the bathroom; it was nothing he had ever seen before. He walked out and opened the closet which had many expensive suits. He couldn't help wondering how a man could wear so many. This place was like the Taj, though he had never been there — it was close enough.

***

He heard a groan, reminding him about the man lying in the living room. A series of events passed through his mind trying to figure out how to deal with this. He had to be quick. Once he transferred into the rich man's body, the young punk would be standing there stunned. Lying on the floor unprotected wasn't a great place to be when a fight was imminent. Suddenly a solution popped up.

The picture was rather strange — two men on the floor with one of them chanting. The words emptied into the apartment. Cil's essence, or whatever you want to call it, transferred into the rich man's body. He opened his eyes and knew right then it worked. Looking next to him, he saw the kid blinking confusingly. He stood up — his towel dropped. When the kid regained his composure, he looked up and saw a naked man standing over him.

"What the fuck?" The kid said.

Cil picked up the towel and wrapped it around him. He remembered seeing a stack of bills on the dresser, which turned out to be $280, and handed them to the kid.

"Here you go. Thanks for the good time. Now you have to leave before security comes looking for you."

The kid took the money and walked toward the front door. He looked back once and ran out into the hallway. The scenario confused him, but not in a *I've never done this before* way. He was in the park looking for blowjobs and now he was rich.

There was a little blood on the carpet. Cil went to the kitchen looking for cleaning supplies to clean up the mess, and then checked out the rest of the apartment. Cafferty's wallet was on the dresser and in it were a plethora of credit and bank cards. He picked up his new cell phone, called the banks and told them to issue new ones since he lost his wallet and wanted to cancel them. He rummaged through Cafferty's desk and found bank account information. He was delighted with his findings of over $200,000, and that was only one bank. Yes! Cil had finally made it: he had a great new body, and a plush apartment — the killing would continue soon.

CHAPTER SIX

Cil stretched out on his new bed, blanket wrapped around him. He had the air conditioner on — it felt wonderful. After masturbating, he explored his new body like Magellan exploring new lands. All was right in the mind of Cil Franklin.

Cafferty's cell phone rang and rang all morning — Cil let it ring. He wasn't ready to tackle that situation but sure, the voice would sound the same, yet he would be different. He imagined all of Cafferty's friends, even the employer, calling, but Cil had no desire to work: he had all what he needed — for now.

The fridge was full with healthy food. There were assorted fruits on the counter and protein powder next to the blender. The spare room served as a gym, with a Nautilus machine that worked out all the major muscle groups — Cil worked out.

After an hour, Cil could do no more. The stress from last week took over. He fell asleep. He woke up 45 minutes later, still exhausted. People don't realize how tiring stress is. He went to the stereo and inserted a CD that was on top of the receiver, from an artist he didn't recognize — Patrick O'Hearn. He pushed play, grabbed the CD case and sat down on the couch. The inside sheet was worn, faded, and hard to pull through the plastic tabs. He broke one yanking the cover out. He remembered a bottle of wine on the kitchen and grabbed it.

The CD was called *Indigo* and the cover picture was what looked like a window with a large black crow's wing. The first song was called "Devil's Lake" and it drifted along like a soft tide. There wasn't a whole lot of information on the sheet so he put it down and listened. As the music flowed, he let his mind wander. He drank wine deeply until the sound changed. Some noises amplified while some dimmed. It blurred his conscious and that morphed into circles and motion; a see-saw of emotions came and went. The sound that he focused on became less important. His eyelids closed, sleep whispered in. Bits and pieces of dreams blipped on the screen, but the sugar from the alcohol metabolized and sent spurts of energy through his body.

The body took what it needed and threw the rest into the bladder, and somewhere in the dream he had to pee — he ignored it. More liquid filled his bladder and his eyes creaked open. Without any conscious thought, he swayed to the bathroom and got rid of what his body didn't want anymore. Then back to the rickety patch of sleep where dreams caught sections of the previous day, things he might have thought, and things he consciously didn't think. Together they made a tapestry of a dream soup where not much made sense. The body rested, the brain slowed, and Cil Franklen walked on thin ice between awake and not awake, but all was dark — until...

***

He was standing on a cliff. The huge wall rose upward. It was as if his mind was a camera looking at him from a distance. The wind blew and the sea pushed on the shore. Jagged rocks below stood against the water, sounding like *whishhhhhh!* The odor of salt and foam entered his nostrils, and he could taste the salt on his tongue. His mind moved up and closed in on a cave. It was far below him; he couldn't see it from where he stood, but his mind saw and moved in.

The wind whistled on the edges of the cave and the darkness beckoned. He walked in. There was nothing but the silence that touched him. It nudged him to go further — gone was the sound of the ocean. He couldn't see anything, but his feelings grew. His stride lengthened; his body expanded. He walked around a corner, suddenly he was small — so small that he crawled. His knees hurt, he rounded a bend and one of his legs fell off. He turned over on his back and tried to feel where his leg used to be, but he had no arms. He slithered like a snake until his foot touched a rock, but it wasn't a rock, it was a snake that wrapped around him, then it became the other leg.

A cold zephyr came in and took on a fluorescent glow lighting up the cave. He stood up and saw a stone table ahead with a boy on it — No, it wasn't a boy, but a lamb. As he got closer, it was a calf, but when he touched it (he had hands again) it was a stone. The glow receded, a sharp thin slice of light pin-pricked ahead — he approached it. The light grew bigger, he found it led outside the cave entrance. The ocean moved and his mind found him standing on the cliff. The sky darkened, he thought it would storm, but the darkness moved — it came closer. A murder of crows flew toward him, he put his arms up to keep them away — he screamed.

***

The CD was done, he had been asleep for forty-three minutes. It was still morning and the splints of light warmed his face — he was sweating. He got up, dressed in shorts and a tank top, and went outside. He greeted the doorman as he passed. The old Cil didn't like to go outside — he always felt like he was the hunchback from an old English town. The sunlight was hard to see this early in Manhattan as the big buildings blocked out most of it. Reflections of the sun bounced off the mammoth's windows, but that wasn't the same. He wanted to experience the actual beams of light — he continued north.

There was no lack of subways, but he ignored them; walking felt good. Along the way, he watched people — how they walked, acted, ate, and reacted when he said "hello." He watched how traffic zipped in and out, and how drivers got angry when they couldn't find the uber rare parking spot.

Cil grew bored so he turned right, walked a couple of blocks, and then turned left. About a half mile up, a pawn shop with its bright blinking light caught his attention — he went in observing the guitars, stereos, and tools hung on the walls. He approached the display case in front of the bearded clerk and looked down.

"What can I do for ya?" The man asked.

"Just looking," said Cil.

He ran his eyes along the row of guns lying below the inch of glass. The clerk followed his gaze and grinned.

"Looking to buy a piece?"

"A what?"

"A piece! A gun! Never owned one, have ya?"

"How could you tell?" Cil asked.

"I've been in this business a long time, son. I know a neophyte when I see one."

Cil didn't know what a "neophyte" was, but didn't ask. If he did, it might have surprised him how the clerk of a pawn shop would know.

"How does this work?"

"Well, there's a background check which will cost ya ten bucks. Then you wait till it comes back; you pick the piece you want and pay me. I only sell them — I don't care what you do with them."

Cil didn't want to look suspicious, he took out his wallet and slid a ten across the glass. The clerk gave him a bunch of paperwork to fill which he did quickly. He spent a good amount of time memorizing Cafferty's personal information. When that was done, the clerk told him to come back in three days — Cil left.

He continued walking for four miles or so until he came upon Martin Luther King Boulevard. There he turned left and headed north to Harlem where the landscape changed from lower Manhattan. The buildings went from shiny to dull and there were more bricks in these parts than down south. There were only a couple of miles to the other side of the island, he continued walking until he came upon the shores of Hudson. He watched the water for a while, pulled out a pack of cigarettes and smoked two in a row. It had been a long walk and he sat down in a rare patch of grass. The sky was blue and the sun was beginning to wind down dropping the temperature a bit — it felt better.

***

Henry Hudson Parkway ran pretty close to the water and the traffic was loud. He tried to blank out all man-made noise and concentrated on the noise from nature. He heard crickets, occasionally frogs, and a few birds who returned from hunting. It was almost serene, except for the damn cars.

When the night came on strong and the darkness thickened, he got up and walked. Street lights, apartments, factories, and the highway shot their glow into the dark, but it was good enough for him. Meanwhile, an old man walked by eating something. Cil smiled as he passed. A few minutes later, two men walked by holding hands, Cil smiled at them. Later, a woman talking loudly on her cell phone walked by. Cil didn't smile. She passed him without paying much attention; he walked behind her and hit her as hard as he could on the back of her head. She fell forward, he jumped on her pounding her head with his fists until she stopped moving. Then he got up and walked away only looking back once.

Cil walked south until he found a puddle where he washed his hands. He walked east to the nearest subway and made his way back home. The ride seemed quick, he reflected on what he did and relished the idea of doing it again. When he arrived, he sailed by the doorman as cool as a summer breeze and went to bed. The New York night crept on — another notch was on his belt.

CHAPTER SEVEN

Cil learned that the New England Patriots were playing the New York Giants. He had never been to a football game, but this game would be blacked out. Since he had the money now, he wanted to go. Easy peasy! He dressed, grabbed his bank cards, and headed out. He had to go to New Jersey where the Giant's stadium was. Why didn't New York have its own stadium? No room, probably. When he got outside, he asked the doorman to call a taxi. Yea, it would be expensive, but the elements of style didn't only apply for writing. The cab arrived and the driver picked him through the city. They went through the Lincoln Tunnel and had to pay a toll. Halfway across the Hudson, they were in New Jersey, where the skanks of *The Jersey Shore* fucked up the image of the state for everyone who lived there. Once they passed the riff-raff of the nastiness, the country began to unroll. In the city of Secaucus, Cil asked the driver to pull over so he could use the bathroom. He went into an Exxon station, pissed a good stream and bought two bottles of Gatorade, one for the cab driver. They went on another four miles, going over a bridge and on the 120 north, leading them to the New Meadowlands Stadium in East Rutherford, New Jersey.

He was early, thousands of tailgaters drank in the parking lot. It was the biggest parking lot he had ever seen. He paid the driver, tipped him twenty dollars and headed off into the fray. Being that the Giants were "home," Cil figured there would be more fans around, but the Patriot fan base was huge and they almost equaled the masses wearing Giants uniforms. He walked by a group of folks BBQing and the odor of sizzling hot dogs made him hungry. He continued walking up to the ticket area, paid a small fortune and went into the mammoth complex. The seat number was on the ticket, so he stopped a pretty lady who was handling a light beer — she pointed him in the right direction.

Cil found his seat. He was in the 14th row behind the Giant's sideline — a good view. The start of the game was still half-hour away and people down on the sideline were rocketing t-shirts into the crowd with hand-held cannons. The stadium was almost filled and it would erupt, according to the guy who sold him tickets. The hot dog vendor came and Cil bought three: they were warm, soft, and tasty. He finished his dogs and thought about the beer he wanted. He took a mental note on where he was and walked the considerable distance to where the beer was sold. He grabbed two and hurried back to his seat — the game was just about to begin. The Patriots came out first; thousands cheered while thousands booed. When Tom Brady ran through the line, a tall smelly man in front of him yelled out some obscenities, "You suck! Send your wife up here for a good time." Then the Giants came out and the crowd went nuts. Eli Manning ran onto the field. Cil tried to drum up some conversation with the guy next to him.

"He's pretty good, eh?" Cil asked.

The guy chugged his beer and looked at Cil. He had a strange look on his face.

"Pretty good? He's got one more ring than his brother. That's pretty damn good."

Cil watched the game, but didn't know all the stats,

figures, and ring tallies. He knew Peyton Manning was a superstar and that many considered him the best, but who won the most Super bowls was information he lacked. During the conversation, he found out that Peyton had went from Indianapolis to Denver, and that one more hit to his neck would most likely kill him. The crowd got louder and Cil looked down for the kick-off.

The game lasted a little over three hours and Cil drank a lot of beer. He learned more about football during that time than he did all his life. The stadium held 82,500 people, they yelled and screamed, but grew silent during the fourth quarter, where Tom Brady threw for two touchdowns and won the game 35-27.

"Fucking Tom Brady," said the man next to him: he got up and headed for the gates. Cil followed him and worked his way through the parking lot to where the cabs waited. He hailed one and told the driver in a slurred voice to take him home. The driver asked where, Cil told him. The guy's smile stretched all the way out of the car — it was a good distance to Manhattan and a damn good fare.

***

A police car was sitting and two officers were standing next to the doorman. As the taxi pulled over, Cil paid the driver and walked to the front door. The doorman nodded to the officers.

"Excuse me sir, are you John Cafferty?" One of the officers asked Cil.

He almost said no, as his mind was a bit foggy from the beer.

"Yup, I'm John Cafferty. Is anything wrong?"

His heart tore into a new rhythm — he grew afraid. *They knew!*

"Well sir, we received a report that you were missing. Obviously, that's not correct. You're standing right here."

"Missing? Who reported that?"

Cil might have put two and two together had he been sober, but sober he was not.

"For one, your girlfriend said she can't get ahold of you, and your boss at. . ."

The policeman looked at his small notebook.

"The place you work said that you haven't showed up for a week."

Shit, I forgot to take care of that.

"I quit that job. I haven't shown up because I quit."

The two cops looked at each other like this was a huge waste of time; how many times had they received calls from a girlfriend saying her man was not returning her calls. The one cop closed his notebook and put it in his back pocket. He nodded to his partner, who walked to the car.

"Sorry for bothering you, Mr. Cafferty. When we get a call, we have to check it out."

"No problem guys. She was a bitch anyway. She took my damn margarita machine."

The cop laughed and joined his partner at the car. He reached over with his right hand to key the microphone on his shoulder and reported that there was nothing going on. They got in the car and drove away. The doorman was looking up at the sky.

"Damn women," said Cil

He wobbled his way to the apartment — he passed out.

CHAPTER EIGHT

Dreams come in all shapes; sometimes you dream about what you've done, what you want to do, and stuff that makes no sense — just your mind going nuts when the body heals. Maybe you saw a rabbit on a TV commercial, you ate pasta, or bought a new suit. By mixing that into the movie about trolls you watched two nights ago, what comes out is a smorgasbord of unintelligible crap. Then you wake up remembering some of the dream and try to figure it all out, but you never can. People have made millions writing books explaining dreams, but isn't it all just guessing? If you drown in a dream, that means you are suffocating from something in real life. If you get eaten in a dream, that means a dozen other things, right? Probably, not. Freud wrote about dreams, which is amazing since he was hooked on cocaine — what does it all mean?

***

Cil tumbled around in his sleep; he dreamed of cars, money, blood, women, and grass. Every hour he slept; the few minutes of actual REM sleep he got tore his mind apart. A breeze blew and disturbed the blinds covering the bedroom window, making a rat-tat-tat noise. In his dream, that translated into a storm coming. He was standing in a park holding a knife. The rain came down sideways and it felt like bullets hitting his skin. He waved the knife around trying to kill the rain, but more and more came. In the rain, a tinted shadow was outlined — it came forward. It was a man, maybe. His features could not be discerned, just a ghost in the water. It came closer and closer until...

***

It was still night, Cil opened his eyes to the darkness, and kicked off the sheets and blanket. It took a minute for him to realize where he was — who he was.

CHAPTER NINE

As headaches go, this one was a bitch — sleep was scarce. Troubled by the previous night's events, he felt like the grim reaper had smacked and left him to his misery knowing he wasn't worth its time. Perhaps, this wasn't the first-time death had come around.

He heard a *thud* as the kid dropped the paper by his door. He opened it, still in his underwear, and grabbed it. Leaving a pot of coffee to boil, he sat on the couch and read it through. The first portion had the same stuff it always did: murders, robberies, rapes, gang violence, the U.N. fucking up, and the president vacationing in Martha's Vineyard. It didn't matter that the state of the world was always the same. Iraq was the hell hole of Middle East. There was a story about the Taliban storming a house party in Afghanistan, beheading all the teenagers. It didn't say if they were killed first.

The sports section was somewhat interesting. It detailed all the games, including the one he was at. It always seemed more interesting reading about it. Tiger Woods lost a tournament and Lance Armstrong lost his seven Tour de France titles. The Entertainment section was the best part. It talked about all the TV shows, stars, the people they slept with, and the drugs they did. On the last page, he read about a fair that was coming to New York. It would be in Queens, Flushing Meadow Corona Park to be exact. He was familiar with that part of town, his nanna used to live there. She was long gone, with her went the sounds of her piano and the smell of her favorite meal — Welsh rarebit. Growing up, he always called it welsh rabbit and for a long time, he thought there was a rabbit, but it was toast and melted cheese. Ah! Sweet memories — she was an amazing lady.

***

Flushing used to be a nice place, but it turned sour the last few years. The fair was on this Friday; it had been a long time since he visited one, the lure of the rides and rip-off games was strong. He wanted to throw darts at balloons, shoot a rigged BB gun at moving metal buffalo plates, and win stuffed alligators and giraffes — he wanted to be a kid again.

The rest of the day passed by watching TV; there was a show called *Falling Skies*. He was really getting into it. The guy from *E.R.* was in it, and although he never liked him, he did a good job. Cafferty was rich — he had a DVR, used to record shows — money did make a difference.

At 5:00 pm, he put on a pair of Levi jeans and a T-shirt that had a smiley face on, and walked out by greeting the cool evening with a happiness that had long evaded him. The doorman asked if he wanted a cab, and Cil answered in the affirmative. Cabs in New York were part of the landscape, and the yellow car pulled up in less than five minutes.

Once again, it was a cabbie's day; it trekked to the part of Queens where the fair was — Cil tipped the driver well. It was the first day and the line to get tickets were long — Cil didn't mind. He could smell the cotton candy and hot dogs; his anticipation made his testicles quiver. When it was his turn, he bought fifty dollars' worth of ride tickets and held them like they were gold — he walked away smiling.

Around the fair, children and their parents walked in a frenzy. The parents held their kid's hands while the little things pointed at different rides and games. Cute little things — they wanted to do everything at once. The first ride Cil came to was the Ferris wheel, which he decided to save for later; there were more exciting ones to get to. He skirted around, figuring he would make a roundabout, then worked his way to the center. Like the children, he wanted to do everything. He was good looking and in great shape. The single moms darted glances at him as he meandered about — he smiled at everyone.

The noise of the fair was electric, even the cheesy carnival music was fine. The next ride Cil came to was one of those ships that slid back and forth. It was divided into two sections, with each section facing the other. Cil waited in line, gave the shabby looking hairy dude three tickets and sat in the far back. It had been a long time; he didn't want everyone seeing his fright when the ship started rocking. The ride began, people screamed, and Cil was in la-la land.

When the ride was over, he walked off the back a tad wobbly. It took a few minutes for him to regain his equilibrium. He went in search for the next ride. In between various games, Cil didn't want to lug around a handful of toys and stuffed animals all night. He would wait and do those when all the rides were done. He walked until he came upon THE TOWER OF TERROR. The lettering on the tower was in all caps and red paint melted down from the last word. Again, the line was long; it was nothing compared to Disney Land, but long for a weekend fair. It's amazing how people wait for an hour just to be scarred for a half-minute.

The line wormed its way through the tower until it reached the chairs in the lift. It held twenty-two people at a time. Cil's turn came up. He sat where another shabby looking hairy dude pointed. This was his second ride and the second shabby looking hairy dude. He wondered if this was one of those gypsy fairs where all the workers looked the same. The lift rose up and got to the top — a hundred and fifteen feet — it paused, then *WHOOOSH!* It fell without warning. If anyone ever wanted to taste their own nuts, this was the ride — by the way, Cil's nuts tasted a lot like copper. Life went up, dropped halfway down, up, down, up, then all the way down for the last drop — everyone walked off frazzled and euphoric.

He did a few more rides before committing to the games. He went to play basketball, but did poorly. The game was rigged — the ball was under-inflated and the metal rim was a tad smaller than it should have be. He had more success at the dart game and won a stuffed hippo: it was small, six inches, yet it was a prize. There were water games; you aimed the gun into the snake's mouth and balloons inflated. He was third from the right and had nine others to compete with — a kid with a batman shirt won.

***

Bad thoughts almost escaped his head, but they came. Cil stayed for three hours, it was sublime. He had such a great time, the only thing that would put icing on the cake would be to add another notch to his belt. He looked around and thought about his next victim. Children, single mothers, and families were out; he was bad, but not that bad. He looked for a lonely person who looked less than moral. Everyone knew child molesters burned day and night, but the night offered a little more autonomy. Every week, there would be a story about a sick man who would go to a park and abduct a child from school, outside a house, or fair. He hoped one of those bastards would be here tonight, not that he wanted a child to be raped or killed, but he wanted to do his part to get rid of that scum.

His watch struck 8:45 pm, the fair would wrap up at 10:00 pm. He preened his eyes closer to the people around. Although most of the folks had company, a few walked alone: maybe some were like him. He bought another hot dog, which he plastered with mustard and mayonnaise. As he was eating, a middle-aged man walked up and ordered two dogs and a cotton candy. Cil looked at the register, it rang up eleven dollars and eighty-five cents. As the man was waiting for his food, he leaned against the metal trailer and looked around.

"A lot of pretty girls here tonight, eh?" The man said.

There were a lot of pretty girls, so Cil nodded. His mouth was full, a trail of mustard ran down his chin.

"Teenagers these days, they dress so provocatively."

The man continued.

"They didn't look like this when I was their age."

Cil nodded again.

"When I was in Thailand, you could get girls young as fourteen, if you like — even younger."

Cil wiped the mustard off with his hand, all he heard was "young girls" — he wasn't really paying attention. He was looking for someone to kill.

"Yea, the good old days. Look at that one over there."

The man pointed to a girl who couldn't have been older than twelve.

"She wants to fuck. You can tell."

This got Cil's attention: he looked at the girl, then at the man, back at the girl, and back at the man.

"She's kind of young, don't you think?"

"Oh, yea. Nice and young. I bet she's tight as a fist."

What the fuck are you talking about. He looked at the guy and it all clicked. *How lucky can I get? I've been looking around all night for a douche bag and one walks right up to me!* The wheels started turning and Cil's excitement grew, like the pupils of the sick bastard standing next to him.

"Not into that, man. Not even close," said Cil

He gave the guy a once-over and figured he could take him. But he didn't want to show his cards or scare the guy away.

"But I see your point."

"Yup," said the man.

The clerk rang the little bell on the counter. The man grabbed the two hotdogs and ate them. When he finished, he took the cotton candy and walked away, giving Cil a wink.

Cil waited a few seconds and followed him. The man followed the girl. They walked, maybe two hundred feet, and the girl stopped at the "I'll guess your weight for two bucks" booth.

"I'll guess your weight for two bucks," The fat man at the booth said.

The girl handed the man two-dollar bills and waited for the verdict.

"One hundred and three pounds," said the fat man.

He said it with a dullness as if he said it a thousand times a day.

"Am I correct?"

"Oh my God. I can't believe it. Well, I actually weigh 104, but wow! How did you do that?" The girl asked.

"This is what I do, sweetheart. Tell your friends."

"I will," She said and walked away.

The man with the cotton candy followed, Cil was right behind. They walked and the man made his move. He walked up to the girl and offered her the cotton candy. Cil eased back a few feet. He listened to the conversation — it didn't last long.

"Fuck off, you fucking freak," said the girl loudly and ran off.

The man got really nervous and turned to look for a way out. The girl disappeared into the crowd. The man walked quickly to the exit, while the cotton candy gathered ants on the ground.

***

Lights from the fair didn't shine too bright — shadows and darkness overcame. Cil followed the guy out to the parking lot. The man's car was many rows back where there were no lights. Cil walked behind the guy and shoved the nail he found earlier into the back of the man's head. It was a five-inch nail and it went up behind the skull into the man's brain. Cil watched as the man dropped and wiggled until death.

He went back.

CHAPTER TEN

The Eye of God looks out from 700 years away. The pupils stretch out billions of miles farther, and the retina's red and blue lines push out more. Astronomers call it "The Helix Nebula," it would take a shit load of time to travel there figuring if the astronaut lived forever, which they don't. The speed of light is around 186,000 miles per second, and times that, well, you get the picture.

The nearest star is the sun. Past that, we have the Alpha Centauri system, and that is a tad over four light years away. If one were to drive a car at 55 miles per hour, it would take a mere 52 million years to get there, as opposed to 193 years to the sun. If one wanted to touch the "Eye of God," that person better learn to go a lot faster.

What put us here? What made the stuff we live on? Scientists can theorize from a millisecond after the "big-bang," but what was the big bang? What about the millisecond before? There's the multiverse theory and the string theory. There's a theory for this, that, and the other, but they are all just theories. Many scientists take the "Zen" approach; it happened because it did, but that doesn't explain squat about why it happened? What was all this made for? And for who? The universe was extremely dense and compact, then an explosion occurred and all the matter spread out. This was a very hot time, radiation was everywhere. After a few hundred thousand years, things began to cool off and atoms became stable. Fast forward 13.7 billion years. We have life, but everything had to be perfect for a "single form of life" to occur. Matter is not conscious or sentient; there had to be a design and an architect. We have red ants and blue whales — there is a lot of room between them.

***

How did indiscriminate matter create Cil? For the most part, he didn't care. When he woke up, the excitement from his previous night still ran through. His dreams were becoming more aggressive, and weirder. He thought that maybe Cafferty's thoughts and dreams might be slipping through — it was possible. Could someone's essence completely take over another? Would there be residue? How do scientists explain the knowledge of one's own existence?

Cil wanted to ramp up the killing a bit; he wanted to tie them all together. He read somewhere that most serial killers wanted and needed to be known. They wanted notoriety. The people he killed so far had no system — no pattern. In New York, the murders were just news that became a part of other news. Cil wanted more, he wanted a name; it would be his *raison d'etre.*

His morning was filled with scheming. How could he kill more people? Where? He was like a child whose parents say they are going to Disney Land in two weeks, but he wanted to go now. He thought about actual cards — playing cards — maybe the second card. But that would mean he would have to carry cards everywhere. He thought about buttons, coins, insects, and other useless stuff. By afternoon, he decided on the dollar bill. That wouldn't arouse suspicion if

he were to stop. Yup, the good American dollar bill —
seventy-five percent cotton and twenty-five percent linen —
that would do just fine.

By 4:02 p.m., he was getting hungry. There was a gyro
place down the block, he grabbed his wallet and headed out.
It was called "Gino's Gyros," although small, it was busy.
He stood in line, and watched the people come and go. There
was a Galaga video game in the back. He heard the
squeaking and bleeping as a well-dressed man played. He
wanted to play so he waited for his turn, ordered two gyros
with fries, adding extra feta, and sat down. The well-dressed
man didn't play long, Cil slipped over to the machine and
dropped two quarters into the little slot — the alien ships
started to come out. He knocked down each stage with ease.
He acquired a second ship and fired twice. Next was the
challenging stage. If you nailed all forty ships, you received
a bonus — he got thirty-nine. He smiled as he worked the
joystick with his left hand and fired ammo with his right.
His score jumped up to 20,000 and he got an extra ship —
man! He felt like forever.

Cil played that game for over an hour. He had to get more
quarters, so he put his gyros on the machine so no one could
get on it. When he was finally done. he walked the few
blocks to Central Park where he ate his meal. It was a sunny
day, the sun reached out with its rays and touched everyone
the same way; that makes people feel fine. The earth moved,
the sun disappeared and stars, like salt on a black blanket,
appeared in the sky. Cil sat until his butt got sore and walked
around the park. It was big, any person would have a
difficult time seeing it all in one day. There would be no
killing tonight as the eye of God looked down on Earth —
Cil wondered what it saw.

***

Cil was already situated in the park by 6:00 p.m the next

evening. Over the past week, he learned its rhythm. He knew who went where and did what. It was his science project- to learn about the ways of man. People did odd things when they thought they were not being watched: Old people picked their noses, the young fucked, and the lonely fed the birds, kids ran around without care. It was a slick cross section of life.

Night fell, most of the people wrapped up their business and went home, but stragglers remained. There were a lot of sketchy stuff going on at night. Earlier in the day, he stopped by the pawn shop and picked up his new gun. The gun wasn't new, it was a Ruger P-90 .45 caliber. Whoever owned it before put on a nice Hogue grip, it felt comfortable in his hand. He walked around the park without fear. It's amazing how a gun does that to a man. For a while, he didn't come across anyone who spiked his interest, just people walking off the day. He wished he could see into everyone's minds — their dreams, fears, elations, and desires. Usually, when one has to work the next day, that person juggles time — time for gym, TV, family, and walk. Cil didn't have that dilemma; he had no work to get to, and behaved like a kid in a candy store — he walked.

A little before 2:00 am, Cil walked by a fountain in the middle of the park. He could see the lights from the Museum of Natural History. He looked at the lights and listened to the fountain, he didn't hear the man walk up behind him. The man pushed him and he did a face-plant into the walkway. It hurt a little but it was more disorientating than anything. Cil turned onto his back and the first thing he saw was a knife — a big one.

"Stay down, asshole, or I'll cut you," said the stranger

He was a medium size guy holding a huge knife. Cil relaxed a bit and rolled over to his left, leaning on his left arm.

"Well, you better get started then. It might take a while," Cil said and laughed.

It was a deep, satisfying laugh that took the stranger off guard.

"You think this is funny? Throw your wallet with your watch. Hurry the fuck up."

Cil laughed again.

"Man! I'll cut you up, mothafucka. Give me your shit."

"I don't have to take a shit right now, but when I do, I'll mail it to you. How does that sound, you fucking leach?"

The man turned his head, confused. Cil rushed, reached into his pants and pulled out his new gun. He cranked back the slide and fired a round into the man's chest. A .45 caliber round is no joke and it pushed the man back. Cil got up and slowly walked toward him, and fired another round. He was only about eight feet from the guy. The second round found home more than an inch from the first round. The man fell backwards, gurgled a last breath and died. For a second, Cil thought about letting another round loose, but he didn't. The sound of the gunfire was loud, louder than he thought. He looked around to see if anyone was there. Cil walked away, tucking the gun back in his pants. The muzzle was still warm, it heated his pubic region, but didn't burn.

He walked around the path that lead east and waited. He heard the traffic and hoped that muffled the sound. No one went to investigate, so Cil began to head off, but he thought of something – his calling card. Inside his wallet was a worn dollar bill, along with other bills. He used his shirt to pull the dollar out and held it that way until he got back to the dead man with his chest opened. If he just dropped the bill on the guy, it would blow away, so he bent down and stuffed the dollar in the man's mouth — he left, satisfied.

When he was almost back, he heard the sirens, but they blended in with other sirens. There was always something going on in the city. He turned right and mingled with others. It didn't take long for him to make it home. He didn't want to go in right away — people might notice. There was an Irish bar two blocks down, he decided to head there.

Green lights lit up the front door and outside windows. He went in and ordered a whiskey. It went down well, so he ordered another, then another and another. Feeling pleasantly buzzed, he bought a pack of Marlboros and lit one up — they tasted good.

They always did.

CHAPTER ELEVEN

Robert Frost once wrote about two roads: one was fresh and grown, the other was used and worn. The road Cil took was like the newer one. His luck spun unlike before, and he acted according to his will, as if the world was his flower to be plucked and ripped apart, but there were consequences. Sometimes his mind was a tempest but Cil controlled it. He felt thoughts that belonged to the former mind leak. It got worse at night. When dreams appeared, the smorgasbord of once tidy thoughts loosed and flipped everything around — waking up was hard.

He was awake when the newspaper boy chucked the paper at his door. He wondered if that kid did that on purpose. It reminded him of something his father told, "I'm tired, so it's time for you to go to bed." The few times he stood up for himself only resulted in a slap across the face, but he eventually learned. Cil walked to the door, opened it, grabbed the paper and shut it. Sitting down on the plush couch gave the comfort from a mother. He took off the rubber band that rolled up the paper and gunned it across the room — he did that as a kid. He scanned the front page, turned it over, and did the same. What he was looking for was in the middle of the second page, nested below a story about someone suing McDonalds for using toxic paint on their Happy Meal toys.

The news of what he did in Central Park took a whole paragraph — this insulted him. Surely a murder in the park garnered more attention than one measly paragraph, but it didn't. Not much was said, just that a dead man was found with two bullet holes in his chest — no leads. It mentioned about a dollar bill stuffed into the man's mouth and few people heard the shots, but no one saw who did it; the police were investigating. Whoopy doo! That it!

I have to ramp this up a notch. He slung the paper across the living room. Since this was the first-time he left his "Calling Card," there were no ties to his other killings. He had to fix that, but not yet. He spent the rest of the day sleeping. There was a bottle of Ambien sleeping pills on the shelf, behind the mirror. They weren't the only pills — being a sugar daddy on Wall Street must have been stressful. The label on the bottle said, take one but Cil took two — he was out. He slept for twenty-six hours, only got up twice to take a piss. The pills worked so well that he didn't remember taking those two pisses. When he woke up, he was in such a fog that the euphoria of the mind being in such a relaxed state was very peaceful. Bad dreams didn't come — even if they did, he didn't remember.

The next night, Cil was equipped with a lot of nasty knowledge he found on the internet. He learned how to make a bomb from household chemicals. He found out what happened when you mixed ammonia with bleach, Drano with this stuff, fertilizer with that stuff, and a bunch of other useful crap. He took the subway to the Bronx with his backpack full of toys and sat on the bench with other people who had no idea about him. He watched them, like he always did, but at times they looked back. When they did, he looked down. When people looked at him, it freaked him out. The ride took almost an hour and he transferred to another train near Yankee Stadium to get farther north. He was going to Bronx Park. He was comfortable with parks; they were a safe spot for him. Perhaps the meaning of that was somewhere in his distorted mind, but it was hidden deep.

He got off at the 225th Street stop and walked into the darkness. The Bronx Zoo was near. Every now and then, he heard an animal sounding their sadness for being locked up. It had been years since he had been up this far north and didn't know his way around. No matter, he would just walk until he found what he was looking for. Since he didn't know what that was yet, it was more a rambling through side streets and dark alleys. What he had in his mind was finding a drug house. He wanted to take out a bunch of people and figured they wouldn't be missed — his morality was thinning every day.

***

With the shadows covering most of his face, he didn't want his color to be obvious. It was a humid night; he could smell the water a few miles to the east. He veered toward that direction because his curiosity pointed that way. The night wore on and Cil lost track. Somewhere east, he heard a commotion and walked toward it. He saw a bunch of people hanging around a dilapidated house. It was a torn up, crappy place with stuff hanging off the roof, the sparse front lawn needed mowing. Riffraff stood in line outside the front door, it was dark and difficult to see from where he stood. Every once in a while, a car passed on the road, and two cars stopped and let people out.

Eureka! The people in line were ancy. One woman, who had her young child strapped to her chest, constantly told her kid to be quiet: *"Cayonte! Cayonte!"* The front door opened and a large black man walked out. He said something to the first person in line and that person reached into his pocket and pulled out a wad of money. The black man counted, put it in his own pocket, and ushered the man inside. A few minutes later, the man who was in line came out with something in his hands. He walked past the others, turned right, and went on down the sidewalk. The large black man appeared again and the ritual repeated. Every time the line dwindled down, more came and filled it out.

Before he made his move, he opened his backpack and pulled out a shabby timer and set it. He then walked across the street and stood in line. In front of him was another guy, so he relaxed a bit. Cil waited for his turn, he showed the door guy five twenties — Cil entered the house. Nobody looked, talked, or cared. It was funny! A man motioned him inside to a bedroom with the door missing. Inside was a filthy mattress and a woman laying naked. She was in some sort of funk, with her eyes open, but seeing nothing. The smell of old sex filled the smelly bedroom and Cil thought he would be sick. There was a man sitting behind a raggedy and splintered old wooden desk: he was calm and well dressed. Out of the ordinary, the man looked past Cil to the man who was in the hallway, who put up five fingers. The man behind the desk nodded, counted five baggies and handed them to Cil without saying a word. Cil reached out, grabbed the stuff, and walked out. When he was outside, he made his way across the street to where he was before and stopped. He checked his watch and began to walk south slowly. As he walked, a loud explosion interrupted the still night.

CHAPTER TWELVE

The newspaper article read:

The Bronx, New York — An explosion rocked the Bronx late last night in a house on Flemming Street. Fourteen bodies have been found, but the fire department fears there may be more. Police are investigating, no motive is known at this time. Speculation is that it was a drug house, and large amount of cocaine and "crack" were found at the scene. Also, a sizable amount of money was discovered with much of it blowing down the street by the time the police and emergency personal arrived. A dollar bill was discovered pinned to a tree across the street from the house: police are investigating if a correlation exists between that and the murder in Central Park, where a dollar bill was found in the victim's mouth.

Cil hadn't read it, he was fast asleep. The newspaper boy was over an hour away, delivering news to people who went on doing their daily activities. When the paper finally found Cil's front door, it sat there until 10:00 am. He leafed through the pages until he saw the article, and read it in a state of subdued excitement, his mouth dry, his heart thumping like the crazy rabbit from the cartoons he watched as a child. It was only a paragraph, but it was juicy filled with details and information. He would have to wait until a name was assigned to him, but he knew that they knew — that made him happy.

***

Trains had destinations, but Cil didn't. He rode it until he felt the need to do what he needed to do. He was getting brave, and that led to scary things. Getting caught was far from his mind. He got off somewhere up north. It was early afternoon and a prostitute passed by him. She looked bad, probably strung out on something. He walked behind her, stuck his knife into her back and walked away, as if nothing happened. The blade entered her right kidney — he didn't plan that. By the time Cil approached the stairway leading up, she fell. Dozens of people passed by without stopping. It wasn't uncommon to see a wacked out hooker sleeping in the caverns and most folks didn't want to deal with such drama. It took few minutes for the blood to ooze on the dirty floor. After a while someone stopped and yelled. A transit cop came over, checked her pulse and called it in. He did that with as much emotion as a seasoned doctor looking for strep throat on a homeless person. He didn't move the body; he knew better than that. When the NYPD came with a coroner, they chalked the body outline, figured out the cause of death, announced it, and bagged the body to be send to the morgue. The crime investigation team did their thing, and a report was filed. After they left, a dollar bill was found taped to the wall near the stairway. It was the transit cop who found it by accident. The crime team had to come back, dust the wall, and check the video. The police, transit cop, and the crime team met in the substation. The span ran from 6:00 AM to 6:00 PM providing a 12-hour feed. They had to run through eight hours of nothing to get to the stabbing. At 2:04 PM, the prostitute walked by the camera and they saw the man who followed her.

"Can we get a close up?" asked a detective from the local precinct.

"I can tell you how yellow her teeth are, detective."

She zoomed in on the man, who sported a beard and a long blond hair. He was heavy, maybe two hundred and thirty, or two hundred and forty pounds. He walked toward the prostitute, shoved the knife, and walked away. The man turned and walked back to the stairs where he taped the dollar onto the wall.

"He brought tape," said the transit cop.

"What was that, Sergeant Hicks?" The detective asked.

"That guy brought tape. He thought it through."

"Good eyes, Hicks. He had this planned. I'm willing to bet my underwear this is the same guy from Central Park."

"I hope you're wrong," The transit cop said.

The attendant looked up, confused. Everyone else got it.

"Why would you want her to be wrong, detective? I mean, don't you want to solve this thing?"

The other three people in the substation looked at her and smiled. A moment passed, then:

"Oh! you want her, uh…"

They all laughed.

"Can you burn me a copy?" asked the pretty CSI woman.

The attendant popped in a zip drive, downloaded the footage, popped it out, and handed it over. A few minutes later, the substation cleared, except for the attendant — life went on.

***

One evening, a young reporter who worked six days a week typed away at his laptop. He had a juicy piece for the New York Times: two murders and a drug house wiped out

— didn't make much of a serial killer, but he felt more were coming. Like all good reporters, he had a "source" who slid him information when it was good. The idea of using a dollar bill was fantastic; it's the first time he ever heard of a calling card in that nature. It was hard for reporters to have empathy for murders in a city where it happened all the time. He knew about the killer *"Son of Sam"* but that was many moons ago. It was time for another.

"Are you working on that subway hooker murder?"

"Huh?"

The reporter didn't look up. He was typing fast and focused solely on his laptop.

"The subway hooker story," said the man again.

This time the reporter looked up. It was a familiar voice — his boss.

"Yea, I'm almost done. I'll have it to you in a sukoshi."

"A sukoshi, eh? Is that "sukoshi" today or tomorrow?" The boss asked.

"Today, if you leave me alone long enough to finish."

The reporter had lived in Japan some years ago — "Sukoshi" meant "a little bit." His boss hovered for a minute longer and walked away; it would come when it would come. The reporter worked that laptop like a fluffer, knocking out his story without caring much around him — *This would get me on the map.*

Later that night, the reporter went to the stop where the murder took place. He wanted to feel the scene — smell the air, feel the tension, and see the spot where the body dropped. The floor was clean, mopped by a pissed off subway custodian who was damn tired of cleaning up blood, puke, shit, piss, and all the other crap people left. The reporter looked at the floor, the cameras, and the wall where the dollar bill was taped. The transit cop was right — the killer thought it through. For the few news junkies out there, this would be juicy information. Most the big papers blew it off. The reporter lingered for a while, imagining the whole crime as it took place. Seated on a bench, Cil watched the reporter the whole time — the game had just begun.

CHAPTER THIRTEEN

Cil dressed nicely and walked a few blocks over to the Irish bar, stopping to buy a pack of cigarettes. He packed them as he walked. *Pat, pat, pat*, he turned the pack and *pat, pat, pat* again.

New York City didn't allow smoking in establishments. When Cil entered the bar, there were six people outside. It was a Wednesday night; the place was almost busy. The pool table had a line and patrons were playing darts. There was a young crowd, the music of Pearl Jam played through the expensive speakers, but the one by the dart board sucked; the bass was blown, it made an occasional annoying hiss. Cil sat down and ordered a Guinness — it tasted better. The bartender poured the dark lager slowly, filling the cold glass with expertise.

Cil drowned the first beer and ordered another. He turned on the stool and looked around. A few college kids, business type folks, and regulars occupied the room. The male to female ratio was around 60-to-40, there were some single ladies sitting alone. He had never picked up women. Considering how he looked before, Cil Franklen was a hunk now. It took some time and effort for his brain to convince itself — *No time like the present.*

He scanned the room, looking for a lonely lady. Some women went to the bar to be alone and some expecting a man to pick them up — Cil looked for the latter. At the end, a woman, maybe 35, sat playing strip poker on the game console; she looked bored. Cil couldn't discern what she was drinking, so he asked the bartender.

"Excuse me, what is that lady drinking?" asked Cil.

"Which one?"

"The one playing the game."

"Oh, Cindy. That would be rum and coke."

"I'd like to buy her a drink. Can you send one?"

The bartender grinned — he'd been doing this for a long time.

"No problem," he poured the drink and passed it on to the lonely lady. A short conversation ensued, she looked at Cil, smiled, put the drink down, and motioned Cil over. *It worked!* The nervousness began. He took a second, grabbed his drink, and headed over. The glass almost slipped out of his hand because his palms were sweating.

"Hello!" — that's all it took.

Cil joined in and played strip poker with women on the screen. Juices started flowing and nature took over. After many drinks, the question popped.

"Where do you live?" The lady asked.

"A few blocks from here," Cil said.

Cil was winging it — he really had no idea what he was doing. She stood up, took Cil's hand. On the outside, he tried to look cool, but on the inside, his heart was pumping blood like Old Faithfull. They walked toward the door.

"Hey buddy. Forgetting something?"

Cil looked back and remembered. He slipped his hand out from his new friend and handed the bartender a hundred-dollar bill.

"Does that take care of it?"

"You betcha, thanks! Come back again," — Cil and the lady walked into the night.

***

The fingerprint results arrived; the crime lab could tell the newest prints from the older ones, amidst the residue of cocaine on the bill. The woman lifting the prints made a copy, ran it through NCIC, and had a John F. Cafferty. There were other prints, but the newest and the clearest had the first priority.

Cafferty had a DUI a few years back. It was a stretch to assume the same man went on a killing spree. Hell, a lot of members from the congress had DUIs, so the link was loose. But she had a job to do, she ran the other prints, of which only two were liftable, made copies, and brought them to the detective. He was sitting in front of his desk overrun with papers, coffee cups, and pictures of his wife and kids. The desk was well used, it was the same desk he had for the past fourteen years. Most of the other detectives asked and received new ones, but Vincient Storch kept his. The woman from the lab walked up and placed the file on his desk,

"This is all I could get, Storch. It's not easy pulling prints from money, especially old money, but I managed to get a few. It's all you now." She winked and walked away.

The detective picked up the file, leaned back in his chair, and studied the results. The first one was John F. Cafferty, a well-to-do Wall Street guy who only had one charge on his rap sheet – the DUI. The second was a punk from uptown whose rap sheet had three robberies, three assaults, and one pissing in public charge. The third was a cop. Scooting up to his desk, Storch opened his database and looked up the first two — you don't run cops without hard evidence. The detective spent thirty minutes on the computer, then logged off — it was late. He looked forward to paying Mr. Cafferty and that punk a visit.

***

When they arrived at his apartment, the doorman was smoking a cigarette. He gave Cil a thumbs up. Halfway up the elevator, the woman already had Cil's pants unbuttoned and was massagiing his penis. Between feeling absolutely fine and nervous as hell, he managed to get in without blowing his load. The apartment was dark, they left it that way. The short trip to the bedroom was spent throwing off their clothes. The two fell on the bed.

Cil laid on his back and the lady went to work. She massaged his penis until his heart pumped enough blood to fill the thing up. He became hard and the woman smiled seeing the eight plus inches. The woman sucked Cil's penis hard, while playing with his testicles. He grabbed the sheets and scrunched his hands into fists — a venomous euphoria was filling up and felt like he couldn't hold it any longer. The woman sensed this, and bent the head of Cil's penis downward until it became almost painful. The juices that made their way stopped and fell back into the void. Cil's eyes were closed, he was mumbling something unintelligible. When the woman felt secure, she mounted on his tense body and put his penis inside her. She started off slow, then picked up the pace. She moaned pleasurably, Cil opened his eyes to see her arched backwards. He put his hands on her breasts and rubbed her pink nipples with his thumbs. Cil's body tensed up more, and the woman slowed down, slipping herself from him and repeated the procedure like before to stop him from ejaculating. She grabbed his testicles and bit the head of his penis lightly. Mounting him again, she worked into a rhythm that made the bed creak. He couldn't last any longer and came in her with a force so strong that he almost passed out. He was breathing loud and heavy, and she rolled off of him. Almost twenty minutes went by and neither one said anything. Cil's mind was a peaceful blank. The French call it *La Petite Morte* — the little death.

Something unexpected happened — he was getting hard again. His body tingled. Being inexperienced, he didn't know how to proceed, so he slid down and performed oral sex on the woman. This took her by surprise, but she didn't stop him. It didn't occur to him that he was partaking in his own semen. Even if it did, he would have done it anyway. He got on top of her and fucked her again: this time he lasted longer. He didn't have a third one in him and they fell asleep.

****

A knock on the door pulled Cil from his deep sleep, the woman was gone - no note, no phone number, no goodbye. He walked toward the door, naked, thinking it was her. He inched the door open and saw a man in a wrinkled suit standing, reading a pocket notebook.

"Yes?"

"Are you John F. Cafferty?" The detective asked.

"Last time I checked. How may I help you?"

"Why don't you let me inside, Mr. Caffety. I'd like to talk to you."

"What time is it?"

The detective looked at his watch, "9:14 AM" — getting impatient.

Cil's mind and body began the long walk back from inactivity to something resembling consciousness. The brain took a little time to get acclimated after spinning odd tales in sleep.

"Give me a second, I have to put something on."

He shut the door, walked back to his bedroom, and put on the same clothes he wore the night before. Now his mind was clear, a low panic set in — *how did I fuck up?* He went back to the door and opened it wide to let the detective in.

"I'm sorry, Mr. Cafferty. Do you have company?"

"Had! I had company. What can I do for you?"

The detective motioned to the couch, Cil nodded. Sitting down, the detective leafed through his notebook — Cil remained standing.

"What do you do, Mr. Cafferty? I mean, what is your job?"

"Moving a little fast, aren't we? Do you plan on telling me who you are?" which Cil already knew.

"Oh, I didn't get a whole lot of sleep last night. Sorry about that. My name is Phillip Warden. I'm a detective from the 11th precinct."

"Ok, detective. What can I do for you? Did something happen last night? This is usually a safe building — I've never heard of anything bad happening here before."

"This place is safe, Mr. Cafferty. I've never been called here. The doorman is a friend of a friend and, as far as I can tell, nothing has ever happened in this building, except the city..."

"Yea, the city. I used to work on Wall Street, but I quit."

"How often do you use the subway? Particularly, up north."

The detective wrote in his notebook.

"Hardly ever. Everything I need is down here. Can you tell me what this is all about?"

Now, it was Cil's turn to get impatient.

"There was a murder — a prostitute. Did you hear the news?"

"Yes! I heard about that. I watch the news. I also keep track of stocks. But what has this got to do with me?"

"After the prostitute was murdered, we found a dollar bill. It mimics a similar murder in Central Park a few days ago where another dollar bill was found. Also, there was..."

"A bunch of people killed in a drug house — Yes! I know all about that. As I said, I watch the news. But what has this got to do with me?" —he wanted to look calm.

"Well, we found your prints on the bill. Obviously, we

have to check all leads."

The detective looked into Cil's eyes.

Cil laughed, "My prints? Shit, there are probably thousands of bills with my prints on them. Man! You woke me up for this?"

The detective realized this was all a stretch. Mr. Cafferty was right — dollars were dollars, they had finger prints from all walks of life. He looked at Cil and saw no deception — he closed his notebook.

"I got what I need. Sorry to bother you, Mr. Cafferty. Oh, one more thing — can you give me a tip?"

"A tip? What? Like money?"

"No! No! Stock tips. I've always wanted to play the market."

"I'm out of the game now, detective, but I don't think you can go wrong with Apple."

The detective grinned, shook Cil's hand, and walked out.

CHAPTER FOURTEEN

It was the start to a glorious day. Cil was feeling fine, like dark chocolate with a Cabernet — he dodged a huge bullet with the detective. He, who began as a nervous man, evolved into a confident and an arrogant serial killer. He wanted to go out and kill some more. After breakfast, he dressed in a pair of jeans, a nice purple shirt and a pair of Doc Martins. With a little gel in his hair, he was looking like a young Tom Cruise ready to make a name for himself.

He spent a good part of the day window shopping around Times Square. There was something special about looking at things which he can easily afford, unlike before. He even stopped by a car dealership and test drove an Aston Martin. The car was as smooth as the shoes —*What was it with the Martins?* As the temperature dropped, and the sun set in the western sky, he went to the movie. It was the 4:30 PM show. He spent a small fortune on a medium popcorn, a Kit-Kat, and a large Dr. Pepper. The movie finished at 6:10 pm. He mingled with the exodus into the fresh Manhattan air: *The night had diamonds!* Aside from the butter from the popcorn swishing around his stomach, he felt like the king of the world.

Central Park lured him in; the only place that made him

fell like he wasn't in one of the largest metropolises in the world. If it was the 50s, he would say he was in a gay mood, like a Richard being called "Dick" — those days were long gone. There was a pond in the south-east corner. Cil lingered there for a while, watching various birds scatter and re-form every time when someone got closer. The water had an arid odor, Cil suspected that it was from all the bird poop. He walked up the western side of the pond until he arrived at the skating rink. A sign on the small building next to the rink read Wollman Rink, but it was empty. It closed at 8:00 pm, all the children had been whisked away except for few lovers holding hands — Cil continued walking.

There was a path cutting west almost in line with 65th Street. Cil turned and followed that. In the dark, like a horror movie prop, a carousel metaled in with the grass and trees. It had seen a lot of bottoms during its time - children screaming and laughing as the amalgamated animals went around and round. Cil wished he had a childhood with memories like that. Maybe it would have made him a better man. He followed until another path led north. White blinking lights caught his attention. He walked closer and recognized the place that sprinkled before him — it was the TAVERN ON THE GREEN. He had never been inside, but knew about it. A low hum came from the place, along with the odor of fried food. People mingled on the outside deck: smoking, drinking, and laughing their worries away. He thought of joining them, but decided against it; it was better to be invisible at night. He watched for a minute longer than he wanted to, then took the path north. Up ahead was a fork in the path, both ways going around a place called "Strawberry Fields." From there, he hooked right and walked till he got to the lake. This water smelled better; it was much larger, so the bird shit diluted better — he stopped here. A bench made of recycled plastic bags sat near the water, Cil plopped down. He lit a cigarette and watched the smoke drift into the sky.

***

Time was irrelevant. It took some time before anyone passed. Cil watched an older couple, from the Tavern, and when they passed, they said, "hello" and moved on. After five minutes, a single man walked while talking on his cell phone — Cil watched him go. Within the next hour, four more people passed, but none of them hit the spot. It was getting late; a bell rang in the distance — the night slipped on.

When Cil got back on the path, he began walking toward Fifth Avenue. There was a stage up ahead where bands played in the summer. Slightly above the stage was a fountain; the sound of water rising and dropping made it sound like a calming rain. He didn't hear the woman walk behind and as he turned, they both jumped. At that moment, something cracked in his mind, he knew this was the one.

"Did I scare you?" Cil asked the woman.

"A little," She smiled nervously.

"Sorry about that, I didn't mean to. I like to come here late at night to think, you know. This place has a way of filtering the muck out."

"Yea."

She turned and walked away, her pace quicker than before. There was no way in hell she wanted to stand in the park, in the middle of the night, talking to a man who smiled like he was looking at his next meal. Cil let some distance grow and kept his pace slow when he followed. When the woman was hundred feet away, he walked quickly. She heard his steps and walked faster, turning once to snap a glimpse —*What the fuck does that guy want?* Cil was around forty feet away when she put her right hand in her purse. When forty became thirty, her fear mixed with anger — she spun around.

"What the fuck are you doing?" She asked loudly.

He walked closer.

"Listen dickhead, I don't like being followed, so take another path — get lost! Go, fuck yourself or do whatever you want, but stop following me."

"There's no reason for profanity, lady. I'm just going the same way as you."

Cil didn't lose his smile.

The woman grunted and said something under her breath, Cil couldn't make it out. She continued walking. Cil got closer. When he was within arm's reach, the woman turned around. She had a large knife and swung it around wildly. Cil didn't react quickly enough; the blade cut across his face, slicing a river from his forehead, down his left eye and over his nose. He screamed and stepped back. She turned to run, but thought of all those horror movies where the woman kicked the bad guy in the balls and ran away, only to have the same bastard kill her later. *Fuck it*, she ran straight at him. He put his hands up in defense but she sliced them, right across the palms. When he dropped them, she reared back and plunged the knife into his gut all the way to the hilt — she ran away. Cil grabbed the handle of the knife and fell to his knees. It wasn't a fatal wound; an emergency room could fix him, but the woman was screaming for the police as she ran toward Fifth Avenue. If he went to the hospital, he would surely get caught. He closed his eyes and pulled the knife out, squirting the blood onto the pavement. He was in excruciating pain, but his thoughts were still lucid for him to realize he had to get the hell out of here. Using the same walkway would be stupid, so he doubled back and tore through the park a little farther south. With every step, his stomach retracted as the muscles tensed and relaxed. He wanted to stop, but couldn't, so he ran until he arrived at the eastern edge, few blocks away from the apartment. Blood was streaming down his face, hands, and midsection — cops were looking for him.

***

With every step, he was growing weak and faintish; a lot of blood littered the way like Hansel and Gretel's bread crumbs. He looked back and didn't see any officers, but knew they were there. He walked quickly toward his apartment. A tad less than a block away, he had to rest on a car to steady himself — *Come on! Man, just a few more feet.* Fear crept when he realized his blood trail would lead it right to his apartment, all would be lost.

The doorman wasn't out front: Cil bundled up his shirt and pushed the fabric tight against his stomach. His face and hands stopped bleeding. Looking back, he saw the blood trail stopped across the street. Squeezing the shirt against his mid-section, he fought his way inside and got on the elevator; it was very late, the hallway was empty.

The two police officers had followed the blood to where it stopped. They stood there trying to find their lost lead. While Cil lay bleeding on the carpet, one officer entered Cil's building. The doorman was back from his business and met the officer.

"Did a man just enter this place? He would have been bleeding," The officer asked.

The doorman looked at the cop intently trying to detect if the guy was serious. He surely didn't want anyone to know he had been in the bathroom looking at the recent issue of Barely Legal: He could lose his job.

"No, officer. Nobody came in. Haven't seen anyone for over two hours," the doorman said. He had masturbated, and was feeling weak-kneed and slightly dizzy.

"Mind if I look around?" The officer asked.

"Of course not. Do what you need to,"

The officer walked in while the doorman stayed outside. If he was needed, he would be summoned. After a few minutes, the officer came back out visibly irritated.

"You didn't see anyone out here bleeding all over the

place? How could you miss it? There's a fucking blood trail going all the way from the park, across the damn street," The officer pointed.

"Listen! I only stepped away for a second. Someone called. I didn't see anything. If I did, I would tell you."

"You just told me you haven't seen anyone for two hours."

"I haven't. What are you talking about?"

"Man, are you playing with me? You said someone called."

"The phone! Someone called on the phone. What the hell is going on? Look! I don't have any blood on me and sure haven't been bleeding all over the park."

The cop stopped talking for a second. His was strongly irritated and was about to blow up. Here he was talking to a blind, fucking doorman who seemed about as intelligent as a roll of toilet paper, while a man bleeding like a fucking pig was running as smoothly as a pair of silk panties. The other officer walked up; empty handed.

"Good eyes, Einstein." The officer said and walked away.

The doorman stood there confused.

***

His body was getting cold, he knew death was coming. Cil opened his eyes. He was in bad shape — his blood still ran out, but weaker. It was hard to think; his body's self-defense mechanism automatically diverted the blood from his brain. He knew what he had to do. Cil rolled slightly to his left and dug out his cell phone. The pain was excruciating, but once the phone was out, he rolled back. His fingers were red and sticky, a haze passed over his eyes indicating another pass out. The number for the phone in the lobby was on speed dial, Cil searched for it as the fog came: *Fuckin' tiny buttons*, he punched in number 3 — it rang two times.

"Lobby!" The doorman said.

"Hey, this is C..." *Fuck!* "This is Cafferty from 504. I need help!"

"What can I do for you, Mr. Cafferty?"

"Come up here. I have been stabbed. Hurry! No police!"

The doorman's eyes widened, "It was you they were looking for. Listen, I..."

"Get up here, damnit! No cops!"

"I gotta..."

The phone went dead. The doorman thought for a second, picked up the phone, put it down, thought. rethought. He didn't know what to do. This made him look like a fool. He kept the phone down, took a ride up to the fifth floor and knocked on 504.

Knock! Knock! Knock!

"Just come in," a faint voice edged from the space under the door.

He opened the door; it took a second or two for his eyes to adjust to the darkness. He saw Mr. Cafferty lying on the floor. Without turning around, his right hand searched for the light switch, it was in the same place in every apartment, and clicked it on.

"Shut the damn door," Mr. Cafferty wheezed out.

With his right foot, the doorman swept it closed.

"Hey! I should call the police, or at least the ambulance."

The doorman knew he should have called the police downstairs. It was a mistake to come up, he didn't know and didn't care what this guy did. He should have trusted his...

"Come here," Mr. Cafferty whispered.

Shit! The blood is everywhere.

"I'm dying, so just come here for a second, please."

"Mr. Cafferty, that's not a good idea. If you're dying, I need to call the ambulance or something. You are putting me in a bad spot here."

"OK! You can call, but let me tell you something first,

before I bleed to death on this fucking floor."

The doorman got on his knees and leaned in. The man on the floor spoke so softly that he couldn't hear — he leaned in closer. That was the plan; when he was close enough, an arm rose and nailed him on the head. He dropped a couple of inches and was hit again — third time worked like a charm. Cafferty used all the strength he had. Muttering all the memorized incantations took a while because he felt weak. When the deed was done, both men lay on the maroon carpet. One stirred and opened his eyes. His head was pounding from the multiple blows. He got to his knees, then to his feet, and looked down. John F. Cafferty was John F. Cafferty again, but not for long. Cil Franklen, now a doorman, bent down and put his hands over Cafferty's mouth and nose; the varied breathing slowed and eventually ceased.

CHAPER FIFTEEN

The body on the floor stiffened as Cil slept long. First, the muscles lost Phosphocreatine and Adenosine Triphosphate which began after Cil snuffed his former host. The stiffness completed after twelve hours and the body would remain that way for three or four days, then it would be flaccid again.

Cil woke up, he was momentarily surprised when he saw the body. It all came back; he was glad that he kept the air conditioning on a freezing temperature. He really didn't want to smell the decaying flesh. First, he wanted to see what he looked like. He knew the doorman's appearance, but he had to see for himself. Cil was almost sixty, but in decent shape. He had a narrow face topped with a good head of silver and grey hair. Hell, the doorman had better hair than Cil did. Wrinkles cut into his face from many years of being in the open, but it was a weathered handsome face. He was taller than Cafferty. Satisfied, he went back into the living room and looked at the body. The conundrum was how to get that thing out of here, without being seen. By now, the building's residents had already gone to work and the doorman's absence probably made them wonder. He made the decision to be in charge of the lobby until a plan sprung up. Holing up in the apartment wouldn't work, as that would arouse suspicion. The police would come back to investigate, assuming correctly that the man on the loose killed the doorman. But of course, the true story would baffle the hell out of them.

***

As afternoon peaked, residents returned and a moderate amount of bullshit was dished out to explain the doorman's absence. When the night crept in, a plan began formulating in Cil's head. He would have to leave the city. The thought of leaving the state fancied him, but the destination would come later. Colorado was at the top of his list. Cil had never seen mountains, and this would be the perfect time. His mind was full of plans and the footsteps of people going in and out became music. The body, he decided, would be left in the apartment. Let the cops figure that out, and it worked in his favor; they would tie Cafferty to the attempted murder of the woman, and all the other killings. He smiled at the thought of them kicking themselves for letting him go when they had him the first time. He put a dollar bill in Cafferty's pocket to complete the confusion.

The next step was to get all of Cafferty's money. He couldn't just walk into the bank and withdrawal it all — not as he was. He couldn't use the bank cards anymore, as the police would track that down. Unless... He could write himself a check. No! How would he explain going into three banks with huge checks? It might work for the interim, but the banks would dig in. Once Cafferty's body was found, the doorman's absense would be noticed — that would make traveling hard. So no, that wouldn't work. *Eureka!* Cil remembered he had a bank account. There wasn't much in it, but he could transfer all the money from Cafferty's into his. Suddenly, he remembered his body: *How long had it been?* Fascinating! He had not thought about his old body since he left it. Cil had no family, no job made anyone look for him — he wondered.

When the big hand on the clock centered firmly on 12, and the little hand slipped its place on the 5, his shift was over and made his way back to Cafferty's apartment. He made sure nobody saw him go in. The body was comically twisted on the floor. Cil stepped over to get to the bedroom and changed into more relaxing attire. These would be his final few hours in the apartment. He went to the computer and started transferring the money from Cafferty's bank accounts into his; it wasn't that difficult. In the morning, he would go to his bank and withdrawal all the money out, saying he was moving to Thailand. By the time they caught on, if they did, he would be in a different city in a different state. When that was done, he put the doorman's picture on his driver's license. It had been a long time since he went to the bank, so explaining the change in appearance might not be too difficult. But there was one thing he wanted to do before leaving the great city. He wanted to see if anyone had discovered his old body.

***

Cil Franklen felt fluvial, like a new wind had puffed up his wings. When the taxi pulled up outside his old ratty apartment building, he told the driver to wait and went in. That fucking kid was still playing Guitar Hero. Something nasty entered his head, he smiled, but blew the thought off. The odor hit his nose as he was down the hallway, the smell of body fat burning: *Didn't anyone notice?* No matter. He opened the door and the smell was so bad that he almost threw up. He shut the door quickly and turned on the lights. The place hadn't been touched. He walked to the bedroom where he lay and saw the stinking retch that used to be him. You may think there would be some sort of nostalgia or emotion, but he was well beyond that. All his old clothes were tainted by death, so they were useless. He came to see the body and saw it. Brown liquid was leaking, mixed with post-mortem body evacuations that happened when the muscles relaxed upon death. The smell became unbearable. He turned, shut off the light, closed the door, and walked away. The cab waited; he told the driver to take him to the nearest, finest hotel. It would be easier to stay in the Queens since his bank was within reach. In twenty minutes, he found himself in a plush hotel with a mini-bar, king size bed, cable TV with all the porn he could watch: *tomorrow would begin a new story.*

In the morning, Cil checked out and went to a Men's Warehouse store. The owner of the chain, on TV, always said, he guaranteed "You're going to like the way you look." It was time to keep that promise. Looking smart, he went to his bank and took all money out. There was a slight snag, as the manager had to check and double check because there was so much cash, which got Cil worried, but all went well. The manager expressed his lament over Cil no longer being "a fine customer." Cil thanked the guy and told him he was moving to Thailand, to get married. It would take a minute before the manager realized Cil was only a "fine customer" for less than 24 hours, but that minute would come after Cil left. He did leave with an anecdote, from the manager, about a rendezvous the man had in Thailand which made Cil want to go to there, but that would be down the road. Cil walked away with a shit load of money and took a taxi to the airport. He was still unsure about his destination, but that concerned him little — La Guardia called...

PART TWO

CHAPTER SIXTEEN

Can you imagine life from another planet visiting earth? What they would see! Traveling light years, just to reach earth's orbit and enter its atmosphere to see all the junk. It is jarring. Our military can hide their stuff; it's conceivable that the aliens could do better. What if they were incognito? They could stash their ship in one of our oceans which cover ¾ of our planet. They could blend among people, reticent, watching them fight over fourteen dollars and a pack of cigarettes, or shoot each other over a parking space on a Black Friday. They could watch a father take his little girl skating, holding her hand to make sure she didn't fall, or see an officer give a homeless man a pair of shoes. Can you imagine what they would think?

***

Cil was dropped off in the departure area — sans bags. He walked into the airport and happily waited in the Delta Airlines line. When it was his turn, he told the pretty lady behind the counter that he wanted a first-class ticket to Denver. She told him a flight was leaving at 4:10 p.m. and the ticket would cost $2,257.13. Cil forked over the money and waited until the ticket quietly clicked out. He had a good amount of cash in hand and the rest was in form of a cashier's check. He went to the concourse number and sat next to an elderly gentleman who was reading *The Economist*. He wasn't one for extended conversation, so he sat, looking out the window, watching the airport workers go about doing their business. He had a little over three hours to spare and that time was spent getting his mental files in order — a new life beckoned...

Cil watched the planes come in and go. When the man next to him finished reading the magazine and walked away, Cil picked it up and leafed it through. It was funny how the Europeans put the comma and period outside the quotation marks, unlike the Americans. He read through most parts of the magazine before his plane rolled up. It was coming from Phoenix, and most of the folks walking off the plane wore shorts. He had never been to Arizona, but always wanted to see the desert. When all the incoming passengers cleared, the flight attendants cleaned for the new passengers. Cil was one of the first to board — perks of flying in First-Class. He found his seat comfortable and roomy, unlike the cramped "coach" seats, where people always bitched when you put the seat back. When everyone took their place, a very feminine man closed the door, and began lecturing on seatbelt and emergency procedures; it was over in a snap — the plane started to taxi away. Cil was a child the last time he flew and the take-off shook him a little. The plane reared up and shot into the grey sky, making a little boy, way in the back, scream loudly, it gave Cil a headache. Soon, the plane was miles above earth heading toward the mountains that Cil dreamed about.

***

Back at Cafferty's building, a nosy neighbor named Gena Wilcox sniffed around. She had seen the doorman enter and exit several times over the past few days — it made her wonder. The doorman wasn't exactly her friend, but they have talked. He wasn't the kind of a man who frequented the resident's places. Of course, there were deliveries and certain calls, but not in the amount she had seen in the past week. And, on top of that, she hadn't seen the doorman all day, so her curiosity got the better of her — something was up. When the sun disappeared, she still hadn't seen the doorman and called the police, who had the door opened. There, lying on the floor, all stiff and alone, was Mr. Cafferty. After the investigation, which took four days, the Wall Street trader was linked to "The Dollar Bill" murders. Fingerprints and the cuts from the woman in the park sealed the deal. Case closed, but with one unanswered question— where was the doorman?

***

The flight took almost six hours and that damn kid screamed the whole way. Cil took advantage from the First-Class concessions, especially the liquor. The airplane's tires finally sand papered the concrete. Cil was close to being the drunkest he had ever been; those little bottles were deceiving. First class riders got off first. He wobbled into the airport with dozens of people standing around the door, waiting for their people to exit. It made him a little sad to know that he had nobody waiting for him — no smiling friends or relatives standing with open arms to greet him — loneliness was truly a killer.

Cil had an inkling to where he would go. He remembered a story about a man who made a big stink on the news when he launched a weather balloon and everyone thought his son was on it. Most of the news stations had live coverage, but when the thing crash landed, they discovered that the son was not on board. The father planned the whole thing, trying to drive up interest in his other business, which Cil couldn't remember. It was in a city called Fort Collins, which was roughly an hour north of Denver. He would go there, but at first, he wanted to make a mark in the Mile-High City.

The airport, Denver International Airport, was a stretch from the city proper. It was a huge sprawling tent-like structure in a city of clouds. Using his smart phone, he Googled where the crappy parts of town were and decided to be near them. Not VERY near, but near. The taxis lined up outside like the people in Somalia getting food from UN handouts. They were in no rush to snag customers — they had people for that. A man spotted folks waiting, he flagged the next in line cabbie, and almost threw the people and bags in; it was an assembly line. Cil's turn came up and the man eyed him closely, seeing that he had no baggage and was dressed nicely, the man offered a more luxurious line of transport.

"Do you have any bags, sir?'

"Nope! I'm flying solo, my friend."

"Where you going?"

"I'd like a hotel near the football stadium. I'm doing some research," Cil lied.

"Maybe you'd like something better than a cab, eh? I could get you something better."

"Yea, sure. *I want a nice hotel, not an hourly whore house. Might as well ride in style.* Can you swing that?"

The man smiled, "Man! I can get whatever you want — wait here."

He disappeared down the line, got on his phone, and came back within two minutes.

"I got a sedan coming for you — real nice. Anything else you need?"

"No, that will do."

Cil reached into his pocket and came out with a twenty-dollar bill, which he handed over.

"You should be a car salesman, you know."

The sedan pulled up and before Cil could open the door,

it was opened for him. He climbed in and sunk into the deep leather seat. The car had a refreshing minty smell with real wood paneling all over the interior. The airport employee told the driver where to go and they were off. Once they were clear from the small airport city, there was a whole lot of nothing for a few minutes. It was a nice change from the typical airport traffic in an overcrowded city. The ride was smooth, Cil was losing his buzz and he took in the sights.

"Are we really a mile high?" Cil asked the driver.

"5,280 feet., right on the nose — not from here, eh?"

There was no distinct accent, maybe a little bit of country drawl.

"I'm from New York, but I'll be calling Colorado home for the time being. Did that guy at the airport tell you where to go?"

"He said you wanted a nice hotel near the stadium. Now, I'll tell you mister, that's a seedy part of town, but there is a fine hotel nearby."

"The stadium, yes, where the Broncos play."

"Yes, sir! It's called Invesco Field. It used to be called Mile High. It's maybe three miles away from the coliseum. Did you want to go there instead?"

DIA was roughly a half hour's drive to downtown Denver. Cil was from New York, so city lights didn't impress him, but the lights here had a different hue and the air was pure. Cil imagined drinking from a mountain stream right from his hands, and if you tried that around New York City, you would grow an extra arm or two, providing there were mountains in the city.

"Yea, I think I'd like to be near the stadium. Anything else interesting going on in the area?"

"Sure. The Pepsi Center is close by — that's where the Nuggets play. There's an amusement park, Coors Field, the zoo, and City Park — all within a few miles. The nightlife is on Colfax Avenue, but you have to be careful where you go. Not all places are good for a man of your persuasion, if you know what I mean. But you're from New York, so this is nothing new."

The sedan swung off to the right, getting off the interstate. The lights became brighter and the temperature rose a little. *There was a park nearby. A city park! Now, that was damn convenient.* He had become accustomed to parks, as they were a great place to hunt. After few miles, the lit sign of The Hilton came into view. The car slowed and pulled into the parking lot, right up to the front door.

"Here we are, sir. You can see the stadium right over there. Come daylight, you can check out the other stuff."

The meter read $67.75 and Cil passed $100.00.

"Change?"

"Nope, the rest is yours."

Cil leaned over to open the door, but the driver was already taking care of that. It was fucking refreshing to be treated like a king. Cil got out and the thin air made his head spin.

"You'll get over that. The air is thin up here. Think about it this way — you will get drunk quicker."

"Thanks! Any other tips?"

"Yea, try some Rocky Mountain oysters!"

"Oysters? In Colorado? OK, I'll do that."

"Not your regular oysters, buddy, but good enough."

The driver got back in and drove off, muttering something about the damn Yankees up north. Cil paid no attention and walked into the lobby of the hotel. It was decorated nicely, with what looked like very expensive furnishings and chandeliers. He walked up to the striking woman behind the counter and asked for a room. It was winter and football off-season, so rooms were rather plentiful. She quoted a single room price for a single night and Cil asked about the weekly rate. She typed into the computer and quoted another price. Cil dug into his back pocket, pulled out his wallet, and handed the amount. She collected it and gave back his change, sliding the key over the counter with her freshly painted nails. She left the instructions on how to get to his room. he left the lobby and headed for it. The room was on the sixth floor and it was as nice as the lobby. The bed was a king with fluffy blankets and too many pillows. A basket of goodies sat on the bed with a towel wrapped up like a horse. Cil's headache had disappeared. he stripped down to his underwear, grabbed the TV remote, and fell asleep to an old Charles Bronson movie.

Morning came and Colorado's sunlight cleaned the room with rays washing over him. He put on his wrinkled suit and took the stairs down. There was another pretty lady at the front desk and Cil wondered if all Colorado women looked that way. With scarcely any humidity, the air did wonders for the skin. Once outside, he sucked in the fresh, clean oxygen and his lungs expanded, making him a little light headed. He saw the stadium a little way off and walked toward it. From where he was before, one had to go to New Jersey to see a football game. It was a huge structure and today's architects owed so much to the Romans. But this thing was a marvel itself, seating some 76,000 screaming fans —*The noise must be amazing.*

Cil walked for most of the day, exploring what he could around his hotel. The amusement park was closed, but its towering metal happiness reached into the sky longing for kids — Oh! If metal could talk. Sometime in the afternoon, Cil meandered into a coffee shop, occupied by hippies, and ordered a large caramel latte. There was a poem on the wall by Yeats:

I will arise and go now, and go to Innisfree,
And a small cabin builds there, of clay and wattles made;
Nine bean-rows will I have there, a hive for the honey-bee,
And live alone in the bee-loud glade.

*And I shall have some peace there, for peace comes
dropping slow,
Dropping from the veils of the morning to where the
cricket sings;
There midnight's all a glimmer, and noon a purple
glow,
And evening full of the linnet's wings.*

*I will arise and go now, for always night and day
I hear lake water lapping with low sounds by the shore;
While I stand on the roadway, or on the pavements
grey,
I hear it in the deep heart's core.*
— **The Lake Isle of Innisfree, 1888**

It was written in paint with the backdrop of a painted sea
shore. It was one of the most beautiful things Cil had ever
read. Cil sipped his latte, and watched the locals come and
go. He overheard two college guys at the next table talking
about a new bar that allowed people to smoke weed. Cil did
not know that Colorado had passed the law legalizing
marijuana and it surprised him. He didn't smoke the stuff,
but a new life might require new adventures. With a caffeine
buzz humming in his head, Cil took a taxi to the park. The
night was gluing darkness and the street lights began to pop
on. The zoo was located at the north and the Museum of
Natural History at the east end. There were little wood signs
directing park goers to these places. Cil thought about
Central Park, where many museums were located near. It
must be the same in every big city — parks near museums.

***

Colorado people were more open than New Yorkers. It
seemed like everyone walked around with a total sense of
security — This fascinated him. Colorado had an old

western set of values. He didn't know a lot of folks here carried guns and he didn't know about the "Make My Day" law. Gun laws were lax, like in Arizona, where many carried their side-arms out in the open.

He walked around the park until the thin air made him light-headed again. Clouds were minimal, the heat wasn't trapped, and the night grew cold. Finding a bench in the middle of the park, he sat down and lit a cigarette. He snuffed it out, after a few drags, and let the euphoria envelope him. Strangers strolled by. He took a while to pick one out. He figured a woman would be the first and there were plenty of them, but his body was old; he had to pick someone who couldn't easily overpower him. One came around 2:00 AM. He watched her, smiling as she passed. He let the distance grow about 100 ft., stood up and followed. She was in her thirties and wearing baggy pants — not the kind gang-bangers wear, but some sort of stylish thing that made *swish* sounds with every step she made. Cil kept his distance, but made up ground quickly. By the time she turned around, he was on her and wrestled her to the ground. He hit her twice on the head, and wrapped his wrinkled hands around her neck and squeezed till her eyes bulged. Her final breath came out quietly, like a faint breeze. Her brain suffocated, her heart stopped, she lied on the cold cement looking up at the starry sky. No one came by that location till morning; by then, the woman's body was pale and cold, and the dollar bill stuffed in her mouth crisped with dew. Cil slept soundly in his king size bed with too many pillows.

CHAPTER SEVENTEEN

Clouds in the shapes of aerials salted the Colorado sky. It was a clear day, with mountain air breezing through the city of Denver. Traffic had yet to descend and the normal daytime noises of industrialism slept further. It was a Saturday, and people slept in taking the day slow. There was no hurry unless one had to be somewhere, but Saturday held the promise of that "somewhere" being the couch.

Guests filtered through the front door, filling the hallway. Cil didn't hear the din of shuffling feet. Spellbound by deep sleep, using every inch of the king size bed, his dreams once again turned sour. There was a darkness, darker than the night and starless sky. He was on the cliff again; the day was gray with dark clouds and in shapes he had never seen before. The rain poured sideways, but he couldn't discern its origins. He walked toward the edge, and made sure not to slip and tumble over. Then he stood, his footsteps gone with its memory. The sea waves pushed and pulled; its white foam slid over rocks only to disappear. He knew there was a cave below somehow, but didn't know how he knew. Just like before, he went from the edge to the opening of the cave — it called him. There was no moon or light to guide him, the cave's interior was darker than outside. Cil walked in until he became a part of it. There was something in there, Cil sensed it. Horrified to see what it was, the sound of wings dusting each other began quietly hitting decibel levels beyond human ears could bear — it was maddening. Somehow a light crept and illuminated a figure in the darkness. Cil watched it move, not knowing if it was getting closer or farther. He watched it for a while, mere seconds in the conscious mind, until its movements became obvious. The sound of the wings muffled the scratchy footsteps; Cil watched it approach. The sound of the wings blossomed into the sight of dark birds morphing behind the figure, they flew toward Cil. He turned and ran, trying to reach the mouth of the cave and...

***

Cil opened his eyes, sweating, he didn't know where he was; an experience most people share when they awake from a deep sleep full of REM madness. The room was pitch black, only the little red light on the smoke detector broke the darkness. It took a few seconds for him to orient himself and when he did, relief spread all over his body. These damn dreams — what do they mean? He rolled off the bed and made his way to the bathroom, stubbing his toe on his right foot. *Fucking fuck,* his brain's voice said and he turned on the light. It hurt his eyes. The faucet was cold, he turned it and warm water came out. He splashed some on his face. He remembered his dreams, it befuddled him. Who was the figure? What was up with the birds? *I need to get into the body of a shrink.* Leaving the light on, he went back to bed and starred at the ceiling until he fell asleep. The thick curtains blocked out the day light. When he awoke, it was after 3:00 p.m. and his stomach was rumbling. He had been eating like a caveman, only a meal per day for the past week. It was what he was used to, but now, he had money.

Throwing on a suit, he made his way downstairs and asked a bellhop to call him a cab. He didn't feel like having a conversation, so when the taxi arrived, he simply told the driver to take him to a mall. But the mall was close by, he could have walked, yet for $10 it was worth the drive. He worked his way through the mall getting some casual attire before heading to the food-court; it did the trick, for the time being. Outside the mall, there were several newspaper machines and Cil picked one called *The Denver Post*. He went back inside and sat next to the candy machines by the three massage chairs. It was five dollars for five minutes. Cil jumped on one and inserting a five-dollar bill into the slot. It immediately started shaking. There were little balls in the back of the chair, which moved up and down smoothing the kinks he had on his back. He tried to read the paper, but his arms where shaking a bit, so he set it aside and enjoyed the massage. It ran its course too fast and Cil stuck in another bill. A couple of pretty high school girls passed amused by what they saw. He figured that he must have looked like a damn fool, but it was worth it.

When it was done, he remained seated to leaf through the paper, trying to see if his handiwork the night before made the cut — It didn't. No worries! He had plenty of time. He only paid for a week at the hotel, but could extend if he wanted — he hankered for the mountains up north. Cil stayed at the mall until dusk and went back to the park. He killed another woman. This one was easier; she was old and went down quick. Four days, four killings, and four dollars — finally, the police caught on and Cil got his story in Thursday's paper, page 2. Forensics tied all the murders happening after midnight and the park was on high alert. By the time the second murder took place, the police were looking, but when the fifth one happened, they called the FBI. After the profiler arrived, they discovered that the murders in Denver resembled those in New York — the moniker "Serial Killer" was attached. Cil got lucky with the sixth one. The citizens around the area were scarred and angry. The FBI profiler, Jacob Miller, caught some slack on the sixth woman's murder, even with tight protocol. Cil knew they were there, yet he killed the college student — he was bored and arrogant. The thought of out-smarting the cops when they could not see him was arousing.

Another story ran in the newspaper on the seventh day. The profiler had the police department leak a little in hope of the killer making a mistake. His reasoning, logical as it was, was that if the killer knew he was on to him, he would lay low — which is exactly what Cil did after the news ran. It wasn't long until the news hit the national stage and high-profile papers, while networks aired the story. During the commotion, within the next week, Cil checked out and rented a car. He drove to Phoenix, Arizona and Salt Lake City, Utah, killing two more women in a park. After Cil returned and dropped off the car, he took a Greyhound bus to Fort Collins. The bus was packed, as usual, and it made three stops on the way. A trip that should have taken a little more than an hour wound up taking almost three hours. During one of the pit-stops, Cil was awfully close to strangling a woman who sat behind him blaring her music way too loud, but that would get him caught red-handed. Resisting the urge took a lot, even with his arrogance escalating.

The bus rolled into the depot at 5:02 p.m. Cil's body was hurting from sitting for a long time. Adding to the stress, he had sat next to a fat man whose fat leaked into his seat. This profoundly irritated him. At last, when the door opened, Cil rushed into the Colorado air as fast as he could, hauling his bag. Following him, a few more people got off and after a short hiatus, it resumed its journey. Cil looked around and found himself in what looked like a modern version of the town Andy Griffith lived in. The main road going through what was called "Old Town" was named College Avenue. It was line with bars and restaurants beaming with lights. At the end of Old Town, there was an old theatre turned into a home for oldies and down the road was the courthouse. He walked a bit south, passing a plethora of young people. He checked into a hotel — he went back out when dusk approached.

***

Walking up College Avenue, Cil saw a range of bicycles unlike the ones he had ever seen. He learned from the geeky looking guy at the front desk that a university, Colorado State University, was right across the street — Cil almost came in his pants. He just entered into a magical hunting ground. It took him some time to find a bar and get a drink, since most of the places catered to college kids. He didn't want to be a creepy old guy scoping out young stuff, although he WAS that guy. At the end of the street, he passed a sketchy place that looked reasonable and went in. Inside was dirty and gritty with people his own age sitting at the bar and playing pool. There was a seat in the middle of the wooden bar, Cil took it — sardined between two old guys. One had a tooth or two, the other looked as if had had a hard life. The bartender came over.

"What can I get you?"

Behind the bar, dozens of empty beer bottles were line up to add spark to the place.

"What's that one with the bicycle on it?" Cil asked.

"Fat Tire. Haven't you ever heard of Fat Tire, before?"

"No, I'm from...," Cil paused, "Ohio."

"Here, have a taste."

The bartender grabbed a plastic cup, filled it a quarter way up, and slid it across the bar.

Cil took a sip, then drained the rest — it was amazing. The bartender read his eyes, took a frosted glass and filled it all the way up. After saying how amazing it was and learning that the beer was made in town, Cil settled in. The old man to his right began mumbling, but Cil ignored him. The mumbling went on until Cil caught a word that flicked his attention.

"Fuckin' president... bastard... doesn't know shit..."

Cil turned and looked at the man, who took that as an invitation to talk more. He cursed silently for that mistake. For the next twenty minutes, the old man explicitly explained on how he wanted to kill the president and how he was going to do it. It seemed harmless, being that it was a miracle the old fart could even walk on his own, but the detail!

"How do you plan to do it?" Cil ask.

His curiosity peaked, even though the guy was rambling.

"You see," the man with two teeth began, "Those secret service guys look for shit on the ground. Wherever the president is, they take care of the whole block. That Kennedy thing, where you can shoot from a window somwhere, is a thing of the past. That fellow, what was his name — Oswald! He did it from a building close by. He was a Marine, you know! Anyway, that shit ain't gonna work now. You got to work on a little imagination."

The man lit a cigarette, Cil followed suit (this place had no food, so smoking was allowed, or they just didn't follow the law). The bartender came and the conversation ceased, for a minute. Cil picked up the next round and the man began again.

"But nobody ever looks up. I mean way up! You see, that's where it's gotta happen. I figure I can make a balloon, clear as the day, and put a little fan with a motor. I can rig it up with one of those remote-control devices, like the kind you see on kiddie airplanes. It'll be small and damn near invisible. I can stick a bomb on it, maybe C-4, and fly that fucker right where the president is standing. *BOOM!* Off he goes."

The man paused to finish his shot of Wild Turkey. Cil thought about it. Stupid as it was, it sounded sort of clever.

"Won't they hear it?" Cil ask.

"Not with all the clapping and hollering going on. This guy's popular with the liberal assholes, and those sheep will be crying, clapping, and darn near sucking his dick. It'll be quiet, maybe I can make it look like a little bird. Nobody will pay attention, 'cept a kiddie, maybe."

"I don't think the president will ever come to this little town. He probably doesn't know it exists."

Cil didn't mention that he barely knew it existed.

"No. He won't come here, but he goes to Denver, sometimes, spouting his new bullshit immigration law. This whole state is becoming a fuckin' wetback playground. We even got those fuckin' Mexicans growing marijuana in the forests. Goddamn illegal, wetback, mothefuckers."

Cil had enough. He made up some excuse, paid the tab, and left.

***

At 2:00 a.m. across the street, he waited. The two old guys left together and walked south — he followed. It was maybe ¾ of a mile down where they turned right and headed into a park. Trees were everywhere and it was very close to the college campus. There was a rolling hill close by. The two men walked there. Near the top of the hill, hidden by a swath of trees, was a bench. The two men disappeared into that. Cil waited until they got comfortable and went in after them. From the outside, in the darkness, nothing could be seen inside the trees.

"Hey guys, it's just me."

Cil announced as he walked into the hiding spot. One old man, who didn't talk much at the bar, stood up startled, but settled after recognizing the intruder. On the wooden picnic table, along with teenage love carvings and graffiti, was a small mirror with white stuff on it. Cil had never done cocaine, but it didn't take a genius to make the guess.

"Shit, man! You're not a cop, are you?" The talkative old guy asked.

Cil replied in the negative and sat down.

"Well! We don't have enough for you. Sorry bud!"

Cil's disgust at what he saw dug deep into his soul, if you could call it a soul now. Also, on the table was a pocket knife, maybe 3-to-4 inches long. He eyed it as the two men cut the cocaine into lines and took turns snorting them. He didn't say much. When the time was right, Cil grabbed the knife and stuck the man, who talked a lot, in the right eye. He pulled the knife out and stuck the other man in the neck, cutting through most of his flesh. That guy went down gurgling on his blood, holding his neck as he dropped. The other guy fell back, so Cil whipped behind and slid the blade across his neck. When that man went down, Cil jumped on top of him and cut his head clean off. He did the same to the other one. Interestingly, neither the men made much noise, and Cil took his time with the second man. When both heads were separated from their bodies, he sat down and let out a relaxing breath. He did a quick 360 and saw that no one was around in the vicinity of the hidden spot. It was a little chilly and steam rose from the cavities Cil opened.

He wanted to make a statement — a piece of art, if you will. He stood, then bent down to wipe the blood from the knife on one of the men's trousers. Only a slight sliver of moonlight allowed him to do what he did with some degree of accuracy. Now came the Picasso moment — he used the knife to cut two strong limbs from one of the trees surrounding the enclosure. After that, he sharpened both ends to a point where they were sharp enough to pierce mangled meat. When he was satisfied with his woodwork, Cil took the sharpened sticks and placed them on the table, next to the mirror which reflected the squint of moonlight that managed to sneak past the trees. Now came the manual labor; he had to pick up both the bodies and seat them on the table. He sat them in such a way that both bodies used each other for support. He grabbed one of the sticks and drove it south into the man's neck. The stick was maybe 20-inches or so, pushed down until half of the wood disappeared. He backed away so he could pick the head he wanted from the soil; it was the talkative man's head. Getting a firm grip, he reached up high and drove the thing down onto the spike, pushing it until it rested nicely on the scrambled mess. He wiped his hands and repeated with the second one. A turn here and a push there finally completed the art. Cil stepped back to get a good look. He completed the job by putting a dollar bill in each bloody mouth.

The night was growing short, he wanted to be well clear off the place before any early morning dog walkers passed by. He was smeared with blood on his upper body. There was a pond nearby and Cil made his way to it. Since the blood was fresh, it washed off quickly. He made his way back to his room unseen — wet, but unseen.

CHAPTER EIGHTEEN

Jacob Miller sat on an old iron chair tapping his fingers, lost deep in his thoughts. He was waiting for a detective to drive him to the airport. He was getting impatient. There were two more murders in a college town up north and they had the markings of the "Dollar Bill Killer." The Occam's razor principle clearly didn't apply here, as the simplest answer to this was impossible — the "Dollar Bill Killer" was dead, yet he managed to kill more people.

"What the fuck is taking so long?" The FBI profiler yelled.

What a pathetic pre-school operation this is!

A man with a hanging belly, several inches over his belt, came over.

"What do you need?"

The detective didn't know who the profiler was.

"I need someone to drive me to the airport. What do you mean by, 'what do you need?' What the hell do you think I'm doing here?"

"I don't know what you're doing here — that's why I ask. You need to calm down, sir! This IS a police station."

Jacob Miller laughed. He knew about the Ramsey case and how these idiots couldn't solve what should have been an open and shut situation. When he first heard he was going to Denver, he was excited, but these guys were sincerely getting under his skin.

"Can you get me someone who knows their asshole from their bellybutton, please? I'm losing time here."

The profiler turned in his chair and began jotting down notes. The detective, obviously confused, just waved his hands and walked away. Seconds later, a sharp looking man came by and said he was ready. Jacob closed his notebook and followed the well-dressed man outside.

***

Cil Franklen needed a new body. He ramped things up a bit last week and figured the FBI would be coming around. Being in a new town, and being boxed up in a hotel room was making him nervous. Psychotic, obsessive thoughts meteored his brain like angry fireflies dive-bombing a sugar cube. It had been two days since he killed the men from the bar and he was sure that the bodies were lying on cold metal tables in a coroner's office by now. He knew they would tie all the murders together and that he had to be somewhere nearby. But what he didn't know was that the profiler was already in town.

When Jacob Miller arrived, he met the police chief immediately. He was put up on a hotel close to Cil's. While Cil was driving himself nuts, Jacob was studying pictures of the crime scene and files from the other murders. Cil wanted to go hunting again, but couldn't risk it, not at this stage. He believed he was in the infancy of his transformation and there was still much more to do — *Mr. Crowley would have been pleased* — but what to do now?

He knew about hookers, call girls, escorts, and that sort of thing. He'd never had one, but that was more of a money issue. Even the cheap fifty-dollar whores in the big city were too expensive for him, but times have changed. He didn't think in a small town like this, escorts would post ads in the yellow pages. He saw the phone book was sitting on the nightstand, *Hey, why not!* Compared to New York standards, this book was thin. He fingered his way to the "E" section and looked under "escorts," but found nothing, then he looked under "entertainer" and still nothing. He had one more idea. Using the same phone book, he looked up taxis and called one company, the one that had a bold line around the ad. A less than sexy voice answered with a tone so bored and plain that made him almost hung up. Trying not to sound nervous, he asked how to get ahold of an escort and if that was legal in this state.

"Well, escorts are legal. They are just escorts, right?" with a bit of sarcasm, the monotone female voice answered.

"Uh huh!" Cil waited.

"There are local newspapers, it's the weekly ones you want. Look at the back page, you will find what you're looking for."

Cil didn't want to press any further, he thanked the lady and hung up. A thought popped up, he realized he made a mistake: If he did what he wanted to do, the police would track him back through the phone call and nail him. He thought for a few minutes and concluded that he would be long gone by that time. But if he took over the hooker's body, they would know who to look for — even hookers went missing, sometimes. An hour passed; another plan formulated. He could pull it off and take another body. Yes! That might work. He could make his way to a truck stop, pick up a trucker, and switch again. But would so many switches in such a short period of time be disastrous? — Only one way to find out.

***

Jacob Miller had been to the police station three times — *How was this psycho doing so much in some many places without being seen?* What bothered him was how the killings continued after they apparently "found" their man in New York. The Wall Street man's fingerprints were all over the crime scenes and it was way too early for a copycat. The public barely knew about it. The murders in Utah and Arizona were relatively fresh; there was no way a copycat would jump on the scene so quickly. Hmm, ok! There was a way, but it wasn't very reasonable — the profiler was stumped.

On the bed lay numerous files about the killings in chronological order. A set of prints sent from Arizona were run through NCIC, the results were those of the doorman, but that didn't make any sense. Miller picked up his cell phone and called the station; it lasted over an hour. The prints from Utah hadn't arrived, but the fingerprints found from the pocket knife, found in the park, matched those of the doorman. How could that be? Miller leaned back on the pillows he stacked against the wall; a story he read in college came back to him. After that moment was gone, he put himself in a daze and tried to put it all together. The only ones he knew about were the ones tied to "The Dollar Bill" killer; that was the reason he was put on the case, but he suspected there were more. For now, he had to solve the ones he knew: the mugger in the park, New York, the fourteen in the drug house, The Bronx, the hooker in the subway, and the attempt on the woman in Central Park led them to the body of Cafferty. The detective in New York, Vincient Storch, believed the case was wrapped up, but the killings continued. In Denver, the woman in the park, followed by another woman in the same park, and four more women in the same damn park. The last two were in Fort Collins and they were the grizzliest. The total, as far as the dollar connection, was twenty-six — Oh, and the two from Salt Lake City and Phoenix.

***

Cil walked around before he came across a newspaper stand with the weekly papers. He pulled one out and started back to the hotel room. The city was alive tonight; hundreds of college students milling about looking for cheap drinks, sex, drugs, and anything else that took away the stress of studying full time. Most of the bars were a mile up from his hotel, but the campus was right across the street. Kids of every persuasion walked and biked their way up north for a good time — it made Cil envious. College must have been great! After a moment of lament, he strolled back to his room with a smile.

Jacob Miller took a hiatus from his studying and walked out into the night. He saw students head out for a night of cheer; it made him happy, sad, and envious watching their youth and vitality — they were so care free. He slipped into the Village Inn for a cup of coffee and took it with him to sit on the bench outside, so he could watch the energy. The news of the serial killer was on every news station and newspaper, but the kids didn't seem to care. It was nothing against them; they were young and carried a "it won't happen to me" attitude — that was the sad part. He got up and walked south to stretch his legs, then crossed the street to the east side of the wide campus. He leaned against a tree and sipped his coffee. A group of drunk students passed him; one of the girls smiled and said, hello. He responded, and resisted the urge to look at her — it made him blush. A couple of seconds later, he saw a tipsy student pissing on a tree. When the kid was done, he realized he was being watched and mumbled, "When you gotta go, you gotta go."

With so much work still to be done, Miller drank the last of his coffee and threw the cup away. He began walking back to his room. Across the street, he saw an older man with a newspaper under his arm and called out to him.

"I don't remember college being this much fun!"

"Yea, this place is amazing! Makes you feel old, doesn't

it?"

The older man was away from the street light, so he was indiscernible.

"Like I need a reminder for that." Miller said.

They laughed and went their ways.

CHAPTER NINETEEN

Cil went back to his room with the weekly newspaper and sat on the bed. He glossed through the pages paying little attention to the events going on in town. He found what he was looking for at the back page. There were so many, most of them were college girls looking to make an extra buck. Labels, such as YOUNG, FRESH COLLEGE GIRL WANTS TO MAKE YOUR NIGHT, CAN BE AT YOUR HOTEL ROOM IN THIRTY MINUTES, BARELY LEGAL CO-ED NEEDS TO PAY FOR COLLEGE, and I GOT WHAT YOU WANT. Most of the ads listed measurements and age, but a few of them had pictures. Cil wondered how that worked; these girls had to go to class and everyone would know what they did for a living.

It was difficult to pick, but he knew he had to and fast — it was getting late. He figured there was a cut-off time before they stopped "escorting." He found one close to the end that said, PRETTY ASIAN, VERY EXPERIENCED IN THE ARTS. He picked up the hotel phone and dialed.

"Hello?" A female voice asked.

"Uh, hi. I'm new to the area and, well..."

The girl could tell he was nervous, she talked him

through like a telemarketer; after all, it was her job and she was used to nervous men calling.

"What are you looking for?" She asked.

Cil twisted the phone cord with his fingers trying to muster up what to say.

"Listen, I've never done this before, so I don't know what to say. I'm sure you hear that all the time, but it's true. What do you do?"

"I do massages — sensual massages, if you know what I mean. The rate is $150.00 to come out, and if you are satisfied, tips are appreciated. I can't tell you what to tip, but I usually get another $150.00."

Cil had been dry for a long time and the thought of having sex tingled him. His body reverberated with energy and he began to get hard.

"I can do that. I have money. Do we meet or will you come to me?" Cil asked.

His testicles were shrinking, filled with little swimmers that were dying to get out.

"I'll come to you. Tell me, where you are?"

The girl didn't sound that Asian, but that didn't matter. Cil gave her the name of the hotel and the room number. Before she hung up, she told him she would be there in thirty minutes — *click!*

***

Jacob Miller closed his eyes; he left the lights on so they would distract his sleep. Somewhere in the void, he knew needed to do more work, but a quick nap was well needed. Something was bothering him; he couldn't discern what it was. It was a nagging voice, the one that served him so well in his work. Now, that voice chipped away at his "sixth sense," it was maddening —*What am I missing?*

***

The knock on the door came as Cil got out of the shower. He quickly put on a pair of shorts and a Colorado Rockies T-shirt. He went to the door, opened it, and there she was a pretty girl standing, wearing tight jeans. She looked Asian, but more Americanized Asian. Cil smiled and welcomed her in. There wasn't much in the room and the girl didn't seem at all nervous. She moved by him in an exotic slippery way and sat on the bed. Cil stood and stared at her, shaving her body with his eyes — he was impressed. She was young, in her early twenties, and her skin was perfect. She had that kind of tight little body he always saw on those "Girls Gone Wild" videos.

"Business first! Do you have the money?" She asked.

Cil grew a tad suspicious: he watched those TV shows where undercover cops would pose as prostitutes and they asked for the money first.

"Are you a police officer?" Cil asked.

He didn't want to ask; it kind of ruined the mood, but it was necessary.

The pretty girl put on a little grin and said, no. They had to say so if they were the police, so Cil lost his suspicion. He walked to the dresser and pulled out two $100.00 bills from his wallet. He placed them on the bed and remained standing. The girl put the money in her purse and motioned for Cil to sit next to her. He hesitated, then sat down. She smelled like Jasmine, or Lavender — he couldn't tell. She smiled one more time and pulled her top off, exposing her tiny breasts. They were just a mouthful, but they looked great. Cil's eyes went from her face to her chest and the girl said, "It's ok!" — he went in.

At some point between the foreplay and sex, the girl got up and turned off the lights. Her client was old, and she didn't want to see. She took control. It had been a long time for him, she could tell. She performed oral sex and he to her. He was rough, not the bad kind, but the inexperienced kind.

It was his inexperience that made it better for her, she moved his head around to where she wanted it to be and told him what to do. Cil stayed down there, trying to explore as much as he could — it was a fascinating world. The actual intercourse only lasted minutes and the release sapped all of Cil's strength. When it was done, he lay next to her breathing hard. She stayed quiet, letting him enjoy it. After fifteen minutes, she got up and began to dress. Cil was not ready: he had not planned on the "after" part — he leaned up.

"If I give you another two hundred, will you stay? Just for a while. Just to lay here with me." He said.

"Is that the tip or extra?" The escort asked.

"Extra, the tip will still be there. Please, just stay for a little."

The girl took her clothes off and slid next to him. She lay her head on his chest. He put his right arm around her and let the quiet take over, but his mind was pushing thoughts, words, and incantations. An hour went by and the girl fell asleep, breathing softly warm on Cil's chest. He wanted the moment to last as long as it could before switching; it would probably never happen again. He was ready, having gone over the incantations over and over in his mind — he wanted this one to be perfect. Luckily, she was sleeping; he didn't want to damage the girl by knocking her over the head with a lamp or something. He left his right arm where it was and chanted quietly. He repeated it three times, at the end of the third, his eyes rolled back and his body went limp. The light didn't dim, the earth didn't move, just a silent transformation — Cil was now a pretty Asian escort/college student.

When Cil opened her eyes, he felt the rush of his essence and power take over. She was still there, with her soul inhabiting her body, but it was under all of him. There was no DNA or physical change, only one mind and personality taken over by a stronger, more dominant one. If one wanted to think of it in a Biblical way, her soul was not erased or replaced. God's miracle of life was still operating, but within. God allowed evil, as it churned the butter mill of human existence. There was free will and the choices people took led them down their paths. Cil was not God, or godly — he worked within the realm God allowed. The devil did exist and its evil manifested itself in many ways. God allowed the devil to do its work so he could weed out the flotsam and jetsam from the fray. Evil and good are inherent in people's souls; they operate like the Ying and Yang, dark and light, this way or that, and Heaven or Hell.

When Cil got up to get dressed, he stopped and looked at his new body in the hotel mirror. The doorman was edging toward consciousness, Cil wanted to leave the room before the man came to his sense. He didn't want to see his old eyes and explain why the guy was thousands of miles away. Cil grabbed his bag with all his personal papers and things, turned off the light, and walked out of the hotel room. The door inched the scant light from the hotel sign to cracks before all was dark in the room — the doorman opened his eyes.

***

At 2:42 a.m. a 911 call came in; there was a senile old man yelling and cursing in a hotel lobby on College Avenue. He claimed he had no idea how he got to Colorado, as he was from New York. The dispatcher sent a car over, and the arriving officer took the man's name and ran it. Flags sprung up immediately and a phone call rang in the hotel room where a sleeping Jacob Miller finally made it to a peaceful place — it was short lived. He picked up the phone and dashed out, the only thing he said was:

Hello!

CHAPTER TWENTY

Disgusting! He just realized he had shot his load into what was now himself. He was embarrassed by the fact that he only lasted a tad under two minutes, but that was minor compared to the thought of his own semen swimming around in his new vagina. What if he became pregnant? He would have his own baby, his baby! Now, that thought kind of interested him, he could pass on his seed, but a child was out of the question - he had work to do. He heard about the morning after pill; when he had the chance, he would set up an appointment with a gynecologist and square that away. That led to another weird revelation — a doctor would be messing around in his pussy, his pussy!

Cil was in "Old Town," he really didn't want to come to this side, but he had to figure out a way to leave the city. He was passing a fancy Italian restaurant when two police cars sped by; he knew where they were going.

***

When Jacob Miller arrived at the hotel room, the doorman from New York was still in a frenzy. He didn't get a chance to talk much when the FBI man rushed into the lobby; he was thrown down and handcuffed immediately. He was dragged and pushed into a police car, then quickly driven to the station. When they arrived, Miller sent him to an interrogation room. He let the man sit in there for a while before he went in. It was a tactic used to make the suspect stew over his thoughts and fuddle up his story. Finally, when Miller entered the room, the doorman was calmer, but wide-eyed and confused.

"Can I get you something to drink?" Miller asked the man.

The doorman shook his head and tried to loosen up the chain attached to his wrists, which was attached to the floor. His hair disheveled, he had that ghostly forgotten look; the kind that children have when they are found after getting lost in the woods.

"I find it hard to believe you don't know how you got to Colorado. You killed eight people, and two more in other states."

"I don't know what you're talking about. I was in New York, then I was in that hotel room. That's all I remember."

Miller opened a manila packet and emptied the contents on the table. He put the pictures in a straight line and reversed them so the doorman could see.

"Do any of these ring a bell?"

The doorman looked at the pictures with horror. Either he was a damn good actor, or he truly didn't remember. This wasn't Miller's first rodeo. Usually, when faced with crime scene photos, the suspect made some sort of "tell." Sometimes it was the eyes or the countenance, but there was always a subconscious recognition — this guy offered nothing.

"How about these?"

Miller slid some photos of the two old men in the park across the desk. They were grizzly, and the doorman grew angry.

"What the hell is this? This is fucking sick, why are you

showing me these?"

"Sick, yes! You did it."

"NO! Listen damnit, I didn't kill anybody."

Miller kept the photos on the desk. He leaned back and looked at the doorman for a minute. The doorman looked straight back at him.

"You're going away for a long time," Miller pointed to the pictures, "You are probably looking at the death penalty. Do yourself a favor and tell me what happened. It may save your life."

The doorman was getting pissed, and he pushed the pictures across the desk with force. His face was contorting and a little liquid appeared in his eyes. "I did not do this. I told you, I remember being in New York, then I was here. I... I..."

"Ok, let's start at the beginning. Tell me everything you remember."

With that, the doorman recounted how he was working and how he got a call to go up to a resident's apartment. When he arrived, the man was on the floor all bloody.

"What is his name?" Miller asked.

"John Cafferty. He's a rich Wall Street trader. But I don't know what happened to him. I went up there and... then nothing. The next thing I remember is waking up in that hotel room with the lights off. Wait! He had been stabbed — that's what he told me on the phone. Yes, I remember that. There was blood everywhere. I..."

He paused and rubbed his head.

"Things are coming back. He said he had been stabbed and wanted to tell me something. I wanted to call the police, because it was him the police was looking for."

"Hold on! What do you mean by that?" Miller asked.

"By what?

"You said 'it was him the police were looking for.'"

"Yea, the police were looking for a man who attacked a woman in the park. She got away, and cut the guy before she found the police. They came by the apartment building asking if I saw anyone, I told them I did not. But there were drops of blood on the floor and the cops talked to me as if I was stupid. I didn't tell them I was in the bathroom. I didn't know what happened, so they left. Then Mr. Cafferty called and told me to come up to his apartment."

"That's when you saw him on the floor?"

"Yes, he was dying. I remember leaning in and then nothing. I woke up in the hotel room. But I think someone was there with me, if only for a second. I think I saw the door close, but I can't be sure. It felt like someone was there."

Miller was busy writing all this down in his notebook. The conversation was also being recorded, but he liked to have a written record as well.

"Your fingerprints are all over the place. You killed at least ten people. And you left your "calling card" on the bodies. This *I don't remember* bullshit isn't gonna work. I've heard it all before. You're going to get the needle — you know! Think about that!"

Miller collected the pictures, got up, and walked out of the interrogation room.

"Put him in the coldest cell you've got." Miller said.

He didn't tell the doorman how other fingerprints were found on the bodies, and how the dollar bill calling cards were on them. This information confused the hell out of him and it put this case in limbo: How many more killers were out there? Were they copycats? Why were they so spread out?

CHAPTER TWENTY-ONE

In New York City, even the darkest places were lit up by lights. Detective Storch, who handed the baton over to the FBI, went about his caseload of murders just like any other day. The DOLLAR BILL killer was not his problem anymore (he tried hard to convince himself of that, but it didn't work). The killings had moved across the country and he was just lost as the FBI. They thought they had their man, but how did they continue? If there were copycats — how did they organize? Who was in charge? Who the fuck was killing all these people?

Two days ago, he received a call about a fat man lying in his own death fat in a stinking apartment in Long Island City. It appeared to be suicide, but he was called in anyway. He arrived at the scene, conducted an hour of investigating and went back to the precinct. Suicide it was, but the dead guy was one weird dude. Soaked up by juices was a book about reincarnation.

There were other books in the room, most of which dealt with the same topic. There were books about aliens, Aleister Crowley, and other stuff. The window in the bedroom was slightly open and it helped a little with the smell. He brought some of those books back and they stunk up the precinct. He snagged the books on a whim, not that he believed any of this garbage — but what if...

Vincient Storch sat in front of his desk re-thinking about what he previously thought was impossible. He read through most of the books; they all referenced reincarnation. Dental records identified the dead man as Cil Franklen, who obviously thought reincarnation WAS possible. *Did he try? Did he succeed?* Storch had come across odd stuff and even heard odder stuff throughout his career — he wasn't close minded. He accepted that not everything seen was real and that things unseen might exist. Besides, in New York, anything was possible.

It was early in the morning when he decided to make a call. If Jacob Miller was anything like him, he would be up fighting to understand all of this. He dialed the number to the police station. The phone rang quite a few times before a tired woman answered. He asked for Miller; the woman said the man left an hour ago. She provided his number. He dialed again and Miller picked up on the second ring. He didn't know how to spring the topic, so he just jumped right in, and Miller didn't interrupt — that gave Storch the ammo he needed to continue on with the beefy stuff. He explained how he found the body of Cil Franklen and even though John Cafferty was dead, how the killings continued. He questioned if they were the work of one person and if reincarnation was possible. Was he off his rocker thinking about this?

Miller listened and took it all in. When Storch was done talking, he told the audibly stressed out man that he didn't think it was ludicrous, but...

"I have to tell ya, it sounds pretty crazy. To be honest, I don't know what to think. I'm not saying you're crazy — not at all, but, well, I just don't know."

Miller didn't want to disrespect the man.

"I don't know if I believe it myself, but I want to run it by you — I've got nothing here. As crazy as it sounds, it's just an idea. I guess that's about that, eh? Shit! I can't figure it out, I hate it when I can't figure shit out. Anyway, I don't want to keep you up." Storch was embarrassed.

"I was up. I'll be up for a while. I have some ideas. Let me pound them a bit and give you a call tomorrow. This may be the work of a copycat, but, and I do mean but, I've got nothing to validate my theory. Anyway, two minds are better than one, we'll get the fucker or fuckers."

***

It was easy to hitch-hike a ride out of the city considering that Cil, now, looked good. He was wearing the clothes the escort was wearing when she showed up. Hell, anyone would have picked him up. It would be a mind-fuck to realize that she was a HE. It wasn't like one of those Jerry Springer moments when a poor dude found out his girlfriend was a man and that the man tucked his penis every time they had sex — like who could tell!

The ride he caught was short as the driver was going only to Wellington, but it was enough to clear the city. The man felt bad about leaving such a pretty young thing alone on the side of the road, but he had family. Cil told him it was fine; he began to hitch-hike again.

Cil finally understood why women complaint about how hard it was to walk in their shoes. He had gone almost a mile when a huge rig pulled up. The sound of the big truck as it motored down was scary, it reminded Cil of a Stephen King movie. When the truck stopped, Cil walked to the passenger door — the window rolled down.

"Where you goin' honey?" The driver was a woman.

"Casper." Cil answered.

He could barely see the driver.

"I'm heading that way. Hop in."

Cil reached up, grabbed the side-view mirror, and hoisted himself up.

"Can't open the door standing there, sweetie."

Cil jumped down, opened the door and hoisted himself back up. Next to the woman was a cat who raised its head to see the stranger.

"Don't mind Squeaky, she doesn't bite. Come on in, I got a schedule to keep."

Cil saw that it was a large woman — not overly fat, but "don't fuck with me" big. The cat didn't move, so Cil sat close to the door. The 18-wheeler rang up and the loud sound of switching gears dulled everything around. When the truck finally got up to 60, it became less noisy.

"Thank you so much. I was kind of stranded." Cil said.

He looked around the cabin, it was filled with pictures of the driver's cat. There was a fan on the dashboard and a CB radio on the roof next to the windshield.

"I've been driving for a long time, honey. I don't see too many girls out here — it's not safe. What are you doing out here?"

Cil thought about it and wondered what she meant: *Did she like girls?* But the driver was smiling a mile, wide smile — he didn't think any more of it.

"I go to school in Fort Collins, but my mom got sick so I'm going to see her."

"Don't you have a car? Gotta be better ways. Do you always do this when you visit your mother?"

"No, I had a ride. He is a friend, well, was. I wouldn't sleep with him so he kicked me out of the car." Cil pointed behind him.

"Men!"

The driver said in disgust.

"Fuck 'em, they love ya. Don't fuck 'em, they leave ya."

Cil stayed quiet; he was winging it and lying was hard work.

"I can get you to Casper, but that's all, honey. I gotta get to Montana. Sit back and relax. We'll be there in about three hours."

And that was it. Cil was thankful that it was a female driver. He didn't want to get killed before his time. The sound of the powerful engine and the soft country music, as opposite as they were, lulled Cil into sleep. Cil woke to the sound of the gears winding down. The driver, Meg, cranked the stick like a pro and pulled off into the exit lane. The big truck slowed down and took a right at the stop sign at the end of the exit lane. Cil saw the lights of the truck stop. Before he asked, she answered why they were stopping.

"Gotta get gas."

She rolled into the truck stop gas station. The place was alive - trucks of all sizes played musical gas pumps, trying to fuel up for many long hauls. Men, women, a few children, and a lot of pets wandered about. Cil would never guess that so many truckers brought their pets with them, but it did make sense — everyone needs a friend, in the dark. Cil sat for a moment, then jumped out of the truck. It would be hard to explain, when arriving in Casper, that he really didn't know anyone there. He would be stuck in a town with no prospects. At least the truck-stop offered outs, so to speak. It wouldn't be difficult to get a ride from there. His original plan was to take out a trucker and go from there, but Meg was too nice — Cil dismissed the idea of harming her. Even a man with little conscience trickled a bit of the stuff now and then. Plus, she looked like she could beat up most men!

When Meg got back to the truck, after paying for gas and two large cans of Red Bull, her passenger was nowhere to be found. Even with a tight schedule, she went back into the store looking for the young girl — the girl was gone. After waiting for ten minutes, the worried trucker put her worry aside and took off.

***

Cil watched Meg get in and out of the truck. He watched her pull out her rig and disappear into the coming dawn. *It was better this way.* Cil looked at the stars for a minute, then walked into the truck-stop restaurant. He walked toward the counter and ordered a large coffee. The scraggly, worn out clerk brought the coffee and placed a handful of creamer containers next to the sugar. Cil drank it and nursed the hot cup between his hands. A few minutes later, a man in the vicinity of 50 sat down and asked for a menu.

Cil remained quiet. He assumed the man would fire up a conversation, but he didn't — not quickly, anyway. The man looked at the menu and ordered biscuits and gravy. When the order came, the steaming pile of white on white with little specks of brown sausage looked like road kill, but smelled fantastic. Cil eyed the plate, then looked at his cooling coffee. The man ate the meal like a soldier; he dabbed the extra gravy up with the wheat toast and slid the plate across the counter. Another cup of coffee came, then he turned to the pretty lady next to him.

"You here alone?"

If Cil said no, the conversation would end right there. That was not the plan, so he answered, "Yes."

The man nodded and swirled his little red straw into the cup which he added cream and sugar into — he looked Cil over.

"Probably a dumb question to ask but what are you doing here?"

Cil retold his story, the man nodded. Cil was brainstorming; he had to make a quick move.

"It must be lonely on the road. Do you have a wife waiting for you at home?"

Cil turned and grinned. At first, the man looked surprised, then relieved.

"It is indeed. What's going on through that pretty head of yours?"

"What do you have in mind?"

And that is how Cil picked up his first man. The man paid for both and they walked out. Cil brushed against the man a few times before they got into his truck, the non-verbal communication said it all. When they arrived, the man opened the door and hoisted Cil up. He slid across the seat and the man climbed in. Behind the seat was a curtain, the man opened it. There was a bed, a TV, DVD player on the wall, and assorted maps and magazines which the man hurriedly scooped up. It wasn't a romantic encounter, but a caveman style fuckarama. Cil's tiny Asian body was thrown around and damaged. When it was all done, the man rolled over and laid still.

"That was fun. Now get the fuck out of my truck."

He reached down to grab his wallet from his pants, peeled out three twenties, and threw it on the carpet. Cil was still naked on the bed.

"Did you hear me? We're done — get the hell out."

Cil didn't know what to do. He was planning on the guy falling asleep.

"Get the fuck out, bitch. If you need help, I'll throw you out."

Cil climbed over the man and began to retrieve his clothes. One of his shoes got knocked under the bed. When he reached in, his hand felt something metallic. Without looking up, he took the metal thing out and saw that it was a gun. It was black and cold. Cil gripped it with his right hand and pulled it out all the way.

"Listen, you fucking whore, get o..."

Cil raised the gun and shot the bastard in the face. Blood splattered everywhere with his brain and skull fragments. He lowered the weapon, for a second, then raised it again and shot the man in his groin. The body lurched up and flopped back — he was dead.

***

Cil hoped the sound of the rumbling trucks drowned out the gunshots — they didn't. Two trucks away, a trucker heard the gun shots and called the police. While Cil was getting dressed, a police officer was walking towards the rig. When Cil opened the door, a much larger gun aimed at his head. He couldn't deny anything since his clothes were covered in blood and brain matter.

Being a woman didn't change the officer's treatment. She was dragged out and thrown down on the oil stained parking lot. She was being cuffed before he had a chance to talk. Before a back-up unit arrived, Cil was bent over the police car like he was bent over in the truck moments ago. An officer went in the truck and came back seconds later trying to hold in his dinner. Wyoming cops did things differently; they didn't take people killing off people in their state lightly. To make a point, they treated Cil like shit. He was taken to the jail in Casper. Cil was scarred, but there was a positive side — they didn't know her from Adam. As his mind raced to figure a way out of this mess, little snippets of encouraging points came to his mind: he was a woman, he could claim self-defense, and he could still change bodies. Guards having sex with inmates littered the news every day. Since Cil was a sexy little thing, making that happen didn't seem hard, so he relaxed — yes, he would fuck a guard and escape.

CHAPTER TWENTY-TWO

The police car drove to the station and pulled into a carport of sorts. A huge double metal door opened letting the car in, and closed when the car passed over the red line. Only when the door closed did they let Cil out. Two detention officers entered the garage, from a door on the east side, and escorted the officer and his suspect in.

Cil stood against the wall while the police officer filled some paperwork. Afterwards, he was "kindly" pushed into the booking area. Brought into a small room, where his belongings were taken and bagged, Cil was strip-searched immediately. Throughout the whole time, Cil's head was turning and turning with thoughts of escape. During the strip-search, Cil had to bend down and open his butt cheeks and expose his vagina. After that deliberately humiliating exercise, blood samples were taken, then Cil was left alone to wear the orange jail attire with crappy rubber shoes. The female detention officer came and took Cil to a holding cell, which was colder than it should have been. Occupied by two other women: a fat Mexican who was passed out on the floor and a young woman who might have been pretty once, if it wasn't for the meth. Her teeth were black and grimy and her face was pitted with acne and red splotches. The door slammed shut and locked with a somber loud click. There was a metal toilet filled with excrement and what looked like macaroni and cheese — the smell was horrendous.

Cil stood where he was, then took a seat on the metal bench opposite the strung-out woman. She smiled when Cil looked away.

"Watcha do?" The meth head asked.

"I killed a trucker."

The meth head's eyes widened: *They had to put a fucking murderer in here with me?* An hour later, a nurse took Cil's blood pressure; she asked if he had any thoughts of hurting or killing himself. He was a she, but those were semantics for the time being. Cil thought about the odor in the holding cell and told the nurse,

"Yes, I want to kill myself."

The nurse took her picture, asked some more questions, and wrote it all down. She then made a call and the same officer who strip-searched Cil took him to another cold cell. Hours went by, the sun came up, but there were no windows. He tried to sleep, but the metal bench was cold and he shivered constantly; so, he sat and starred at the white wall. A few hours later, the officers put Cil into a pod upstairs. There were three pods each having 15 rooms, shared by two. Inside each room was a bunk-bed, a toilet, sink, and a metal desk. Cil was alone. He took the top bunk and tried to get some sleep. The cushion was thin — so was the pillow. A tag on the mattress had one single word — BARKER. Cil pulled the army blanket over him and drifted away.

It's strange how peaceful incarceration can be: four walls, a bed, and a toilet, nothing else. There is nowhere to go, and that can be refreshing. Cil slept all day. At night, he remained in his bed, thinking. He didn't have to worry about getting caught, about food, or a place to stay. The only thing he HAD to worry about was getting out, and that plan was simmering on the front burner. It was quiet for most of the day, except for the occasional laugh or angry yell. For the first time, Cil didn't feel stranded; he thought how it might be for a baby in a crib, with nowhere to go, Cil was in no hurry — yet.

***

There was a clamor in the general population area, Cil jumped out from his top bunk and went to the door — it was open. Outside, inmates were standing in line near the observation room. It was dinner time. He left his cell and joined the women in line. The smell was horrible. He was glad he slept through lunch. In the line, trays were given out and assorted crap was put on them. Compartments were fill with meat mixture, limp vegetables, and a piece of white bread thrown on top of the smorgasbord. Cil took his tray and sat in front of a table next to his room. There were two other women. One looked up briefly and went back to the cuisine. Cil followed suit and didn't attempt to make conversation. When the meal was done, another line formed. The trays were emptied into large plastic trash cans and the inmates went about cleaning the pod. Once the cleaning was done, two TVs were turned on and most of the inmates sat in front of them. Some congregated at the tables, played cards, while others talked.

Cil went back to his room, and in less than ten minutes a guard came and handed her a piece of paper.

"What's this?" Cil asked.

"You'll see the judge tomorrow at 8:00 AM. Make sure you're up." The guard responded.

"But, what...?"

"It's all on the paper I just gave you." The guard left without saying anything else.

When Cil arrived at the jail, he didn't corporate - not because he didn't want to, but because he couldn't. They asked for his name, social security number, and birthday but he didn't know. He was listed as "Jane Doe." Along with the other important information was the time and date set to appear before the judge — that was it. Cil set the paper on the desk and climbed back into his bed; he fell asleep quickly. Soon, the doors locked, the noise simmered down, and the lights went out; the inmates at Casper County Jail slept through another night.

***

The morning din opened Cil's eyes: doors unlocked, the female inmates tiredly slumped into the common area to line up for breakfast — powdered eggs and more mystery meat accented with a piece of white bread. After breakfast, Cil, along with eight other women, were walked, bound by cuffs and chains, to a viewing room in the adjacent building. That was where the close circuit television would be and where Cil would see the judge. He sat with the other riff-raff while the male and female guards stood throughout the room and the doorway. The TV was on and the necessary connections were made for the link to be established. Soon, a picture of the judge's desk came into view. Then two guards entered the room, they were followed by two clerks who sat on each side of the judge's seat. They went about scurrying through files and putting them in order. After an hour, the judge came in and sat down, and the low talk among the women in jail quickly hushed as the judge turned on his microphone. He tested it, spoke to the clerks beside him — the man did not look happy.

When the judge had his paperwork in order, he nodded to the clerk to his left and the morning's docket began. First, the judge went on explaining to the inmates their rights and their right to an attorney. Then the judge explained the different pleas the inmates could cop. He read down the list and Cil decided on the "not guilty" plea, but he was guilty — guilty as hell. He needed more time and a trial would afford him that. When all the legal stuff was done, the judge called the first person.

The first was an illegal immigrant from Mexico. She jumped the border a little over two weeks ago and got caught stealing lipstick from the local Walmart. A translator was brought in and the woman pleaded guilty. The judge explained how ICE could pick her for an immigration violation and the woman nodded, but she knew nothing would be done. Her sentence was two weeks in jail and a $150.00 fine. The next inmate was also an illegal immigrant and her crime was speeding. The judge gave her the same spiel and a $300.00 fine. Neither woman could pay, so they both nodded and moved on through the system. Then came the local inmates: six were called before Cil, including the meth head from earlier. It was the woman's third time and she was put in prison for a long time. This judge didn't take any crap and Cil was getting nervous, but all in all, prison would not be much different than jail —but harder to get out.

The judge called "Jane Doe." Cil stood and approached the camera and microphone. He had seen various counselors and jail-type staff, the answer was the same — he didn't know her name.

"Are you pleading the 5th?" The judge asked.

"I have to, I guess. I really don't know who I am." Cil answered.

The judge shook his head and wrote something in the file. Then motioned for one of the deputies.

"Has she been printed?"

"Yes sir, we don't have anything yet, but we are working on it."

"I'm going to set up a continuance and when the prints come back, bring her. Until then, she'll stay with you."

The judge closed the file and called the next name. Cil sat back down and watched the other four women. Three hours later, they were led back to jail and put in lock-down. Two of the women were released, and later that day, Cil had a cellmate. The prints came back the next day and Cil found out he was Sara Cho, a student at CSU who screwed men on the side — now, the ball would begin rolling.

CHAPTER TWENTY-THREE

The next 10 days passed on uneventfully. Cil went back to see the judge in the actual court (that was embarrassing, as he had to be transported by van and still in the orange jumpsuit) and pleaded "not guilty" — the judge smirked. Cil was told that the evidence was mountainous: the truck stop had cameras outside, they showed Cil getting in and out of the truck; the cop who took Cil into custody saw the blood all over her body, and Cil told the meth head he did it, yet the system was the system — a trial was set. The D.A. had the case in the bag. When Cil's public defender tried to cop a plea, The D.A. told the man, "No way in hell." The public defender tried the temporary insanity act, but no one bought that. With a jury selected, the trial was 29 days away — Cil got busy.

In the meantime, Cil slept, ate jail food, cleaned, and watched a little TV. His cellmate was a woman who repeatedly beat-up her husband but this time, she pulled a knife on the guy. Like before, he didn't press charges, but she was a habitual offender and the judge thought a month in jail might do some good. Other than her hatred for her husband, she was a somewhat nice lady. Cil talked with her about men, life, and how to suck a dick properly — life went on behind the bars.

Jacob Miller was at a stand-still. The killings had stopped and he still had nothing. When he reported "nothing" back to Denver, they called him back. It was no use wasting resources and time — he wasn't pleased. Though he focused on other cases, he kept an eye on this one.

It was a typical, fluorescently lit day. Cil and his roommate were sitting in their bunks talking about whatever came up. The trial was approaching fast and Cil had to get a plan going. At first, he was being picky with the guard, but time was getting short. It was time to pick a man. He had to be older, somewhat desperate, and lonely. There were a few, but most of the guards were young males with a few young females sprinkled in.

"What do you think about Haggard?" Cil asked his roommate.

"Who?"

"Haggard, the guard with the goatee."

"Most of the guards have goatees, don't they? Are you talking about the nice one?"

"Yea, he's pretty fine, eh? He treats everyone all right. You can tell he works out."

"He's like fifty. You like older guys? Maybe I can hook you up with my fucking no-good husband. He likes the young stuff."

They both laughed.

Cil had to figure out a way to get the guard isolated so he could flirt with him. He usually worked the night shift so they didn't see him a lot, but there were chances right after dinner. It was the middle of the day, an hour away from lunch. Cil and Tabitha, his roommate, laid on their bunks shooting the breeze until the doors unlocked. Lunch was being delivered from downstairs. They stood aside, letting other women line up, then grabbed their lunches and went into the open area. The meal was terrible, as usual, consisting of really nasty meat and fake cheese. This time they had coffee and a cookie for dessert, which was rare. Cil ate his lunch while Tabitha talked about her life. It was a shitty life with trailer parks and cheating — ideal for a Jerry Springer show.

The inmates were allowed to play until dinner. Most of them played cards and watched TV. Some read while others sat in their cells waiting for the misery to end. After dinner, they had an hour before lockdown and then the lights went dim. Haggard came at 6:00 p.m., right after dinner. While the women were cleaning the pod, Cil walked up to the guard and struck a conversation. He learned much from Tabitha on how to flirt. It was like the scene in Fast Times at Ridgemont High, where Phoebe Cates taught her friend how to give a blowjob using a hotdog. Cil threw on the charm. Haggard, a widower, had been alone for a long time. He went to work, came home, slept, and went back to work — that was his life.

The first flirting session was quaint - dropped eyes and cute conversation. The guard scratched every surface he could to find to sound cool, but knew he came off as lame. On his way home, he went through the whole episode in his mind. He pinpointed where he sounded stupid and where he might have been cool — he concluded that he was lame the whole time. Oh, well! She was just an inmate and way too young.

***

It was two days before anything significant happened. There was a shower in every pod, consisting of a tiny enclosed space with a shabby curtain. It was on the bottom floor situated between two cells. The curtain was a generic black — not the Martha Stewart kind, but the Walmart special that cost ten bucks. It was covered in soap scum and dried funk. Cil forgot to bring his soap and had to use the nasty, pubic hair polluted soap already on the floor, but he washed it off well. He was washing his face when he saw a movement. He wrinkled the curtain back an inch and saw two women standing on both sides. Suspecting nothing, he went back to cleaning. They must have been waiting for their turn. But the curtain opened and a large tattooed woman entered.

"Hey!"

"Shut up, bitch! Scream and I'll fuck you up."

The woman closed the curtain and pulled down her orange pants. She wasn't wearing a jumpsuit. Cil didn't know what to do, but remained quiet. This chick had a bad reputation. The big woman dropped her underwear.

"Eat it."

"Huh?" Cil asked.

"Eat my pussy, bitch!"

"Fuck you!" Cil said

He tried to get out, but the behemoth blocked his way — she smiled.

"The guards won't protect you all the time. I'll get to you, I get to everyone. You can do it here or somewhere else, but you will eat my pussy."

Cil stood, naked and dripping. One of the girls outside pawed at the curtain, alerting the Head Bitch — a guard was nearing. The large tattooed woman put her dirty hand over Cil's mouth and a sharpened toothbrush against Cil's neck. A shadow passed in front of the curtain, Cil stayed silent.

"Why are you standing here?" The guard asked the two outside.

The pointed toothbrush dug in a little deeper into Cil's soft neck.

"Waiting for our turn, sir," The woman on the left answered.

Cil couldn't see, but the guard looked at the two women and smiled. He knew what was happening and could have done something, but didn't. The political workings of a jail weren't always dictated by the guards — at times, its essential to let Romans do what they do. The man passed, one of the girls outside said the coast was clear.

"Good girl! You're learning. Now, get to work — it's not that bad."

The large woman eased up her weapon, and Cil went down. There was no way around it; he didn't want to die naked in a shower. Cil wasn't very experienced, but muscle memory kicked in. Cil's tongue darted in and out of the woman's vulva expertly. He wrapped his hands around the big woman's legs and butt, and sucked in the clitoris. He bit it gently while glossing over it with his tongue. The large woman moaned, pressing Cil's head into her patch which was hairy and unkempt. Cil worked on that thing for five minutes until his tormentor yanked her head away and slammed it against the wall.

"Now that you've been in, you'll want to come back again. That's enough for today. Stay warm, bitch! I'll be calling you."

She pulled up her pants, and walked away with her two body guards. Cil waited until her nose stop bleeding and exited the shower — when she did, everyone in the pod stared at her.

***

The next seven days continued to get worse, yet Cil pressed on with his flirtations with the nice guard. He added something new to his agenda; he planned to kill that bitch. She raped her on the fourth day, after the shower encounter, with a make-shift dildo made from a broken mop handle. The broken end wasn't used, but the pain was immense. Cil's hatred with his motivation to get out grew and desperation ramped things up.

On Monday, Cil had a pre-trial conference with an assistant D.A., along with his public defender. It only took half an hour, and the outlook didn't look good. Even his court appointed lawyer was sullen. He sat and listened to the offers and let the suits do the talking. His attorney led out with a Temporary Insanity plea, but the district attorney blew that off right away. It was to be a First-Degree Murder and nothing else. *Why have a fucking lawyer?* — he looked at the white wall. The D.A. was going for the death penalty and Cil's public defender informed that he would probably get it — that was for the jury to decide. The jury would be made up of local people, who lived in the area, and some of them might be truckers. Yup, Cil would drink the deadly juice and his body would be buried in a graveyard without flowers.

Cil's eyes were wide open when the lights turned on the next morning. While everyone ate, he stayed on his bunk with his mind racing, so much, that he didn't realize his cellmate came in. He was so close to disclosing his plan — no biggie! She wouldn't believe him.

CHAPTER TWENTY-FOUR

He let out the story like a slow fishing line, reeling in a dumbfounded woman with bits and pieces from here and there. *It was bunk, but it was interesting bunk* — she listened all the way through. Cil began at the beginning and told the tale chronologically, ending with him being arrested at the truck-stop. When he finished, the silence took minutes to break.

"Are you shitting me?" His cellmate asked.

She was leaning on her right arm against the wall.

"No, it will happen soon. They are going to kill me for this. I'm getting out."

Cil couldn't see it, but Tabitha rolled her eyes and straightened out on the bed.

"Well, good luck with that. Maybe, I'll see you on the outside someday, eh?"

A low chuckle rumbled the bed.

Cil didn't care about her not believing him — Hell, it worked better that way. But the story had to come out; it was eating him up. He felt relieved and fresh. Later that night, Cil went to the guard, who he zeroed in on, and told that he felt sick. Cil let out that he had been made to eat a bar of soap by the mean bitch and that his stomach was on fire. The guard, who liked her, escorted Cil to the nurse — the game was on. They walked along the corridor on the red line, down the middle, and took a right by the elevator. Then, they had to walk another hundred feet or so to the locked door only the guards could open.

"How long has it been?" Cil asked.

"Excuse me?"

He didn't hear the question as he was coincidently thinking of what it would be like to see her naked.

"How long has it been since you had sex?"

The guard stopped and put a hand on Cil's shoulder. He turned and looked at Cil in the eyes and smiled. It was a gentle smile with no malevolence whatsoever.

"How old are you?" He asked.

"Twenty-two."

The guard laughed a bit, "You were around three or four the last time. Puts things into perspective, doesn't it?"

Cil grabbed the man's right hand, "Where can we go?"

"Are you proposing what I think you are proposing?"

Cil leaned up and whispered something in the guard's ear; it made the old man turn red. The answer to the question was dirty and desire built in the dryness of the guard's loins. Something moved, and it wasn't the elevated heartbeat. There was a closet up to the right, maybe 50 feet from the locked door and the guard escorted Cil to it. He pulled out his rattling key chain and looked for a key to open the cleaning supplies room. He went through half a dozen before he found it and opened the door quickly. Cil darted in first and pulled the guard in, who shut the door. There was a bucket on the floor, Cil stepped on it producing a loud sound.

"*Shhhhhhh!* If we get caught, I'll get fired on the spot and probably join you here in this building."

Cil slowly took his foot out of the bucket while the guard turned the light on and abruptly shut it off again. If someone walked by and saw the light on, well, that wouldn't be good.

"We don't need that." Cil said

He began fumbling with the guard's belt. Once it loosened, Cil lowered the man's pants and underwear.

"It's been a long time." Haggard said.

His penis twitched to an erection and his breathing became heavy. Cil took his manhood into her mouth. A few seconds later, Haggard tensed up, so Cil slowed down. Then he bent the guard's penis slightly at the tip and waited until the dogs of war simmered down. Cil removed her pants and underwear, dropping them on the bleached floor. He pulled up his right leg and wrapped it around Haggard's waist, guiding the man in. It started slowly and within seconds the rhythm picked up. Cil let the guard thrust into her dictating the pace, and when he felt the guard was ready to release, she reached back and stuck her middle finger into his rectum. The man froze for a second, then exhaled loudly while he came. Cil held on, while the guard's body convulsed — it was done.

Cil brought her leg down and began to dress herself. Haggard fell back to the wall, knocking a mop off its handle. He fainted. Cil finished dressing and listened to the man breathing. When he felt he had it, he quickly went over the incantations in his mind and murmured the words loud enough to do the trick. Like before, there was a transfusion in action when one person's essence floated across a little bit of time and space into another's. Within seconds, it was complete — Cil opened his eyes to a familiar darkness.

***

Sara Cho stepped into the bucket again; it made a tremendous amount of noise. Groggy, but alert, Cil reached out, grabbed the girl's head and threw it against the opposite wall. She slid down and crumbled on the floor. Cil turned on the light. He watched the pretty thing breathe, got dressed, turned off the light, and exited the closet. She would eventually be found. Bits and pieces of the guard's knowledge seeped into Cil's consciousness, but they were thin and sinewy. The stuff he needed hadn't come yet, he hopep it would by the time he prepared to leave the iron doors. No matter — winging it was becoming a science to him.

When he left the closet, he turned right and made for the locked door. He'd been down this road before and knew there was a camera right above the door. He looked up at the lens and smiled. Like magic, the door creaked and slid open. There was another hallway with offices lined up on both sides. He continued straight, which brought him to another door. Like the last time, this too opened. He was now in the booking area. There were half a dozen inmates waiting to be processed. A really drunk guy was being fingerprinted by the front desk; it took two detention officers to hold him up. There were a handful of officers busy with their duties. Cil walked up to the big, ex-Marine looking lady behind the main desk. He was about to speak, but something grainy slid across his brain. The processing guard watched him as he searched his mind for the thing bugging him. Seconds passed, Cil straightened up — his face contorted back into shape.

"I'll be right back. Gotta take care of something real quick, then I'm going out for Chinese. If you want, I'll pick up something for you"

He began to walk away.

"Wait, which one?" The guard asked.

How could she know?

"Huh?"

"Which Chinese place? Changs?"

"Yup."

Cil walked back the same way he came. The inmates had finished cleaning and were going about their pre-lockdown business. Cil went to the security room and told the guard the nurse wanted to see the inmate responsible for making

Sara Cho eat the soap. The man nodded and went back to his computer game. Cil saw the mean bitch playing spades with her flock and told her to come with him. It was a chance to get out of the pod so the woman went agreeably. Cil led her down the hall. When they got to the closet, he stopped.

"Hold on, I've got a stash of smokes in here. You want one?"

"Are you trying to trap me? Fuck no! Take me to the damn nurse."

"Ok, but I'm going to get one."

He opened the door and pushed the woman in, hurrying in after her. Without turning on the light, he wrapped his hands around the woman's neck and chocked the life out of her — then he raped her. Then he smacked Sara Cho's head into the wall again.

As he walked out, a huge smile was spreading across his face. The lights were shutting off in all the pods and the inmates were climbing into their bunks. It wouldn't be long until they did a head-count and found two inmates missing from Pod 3-D, but Cil didn't care; he had a new car and a gun.

He was free.

CHAPTER TWENTY-FIVE

As Cil was driving, east out of Casper, a head-count took place. The jail was locked down and a search initiated to find the two missing inmates. Every door was checked and double checked. When they opened the door to the cleaning closet — the shit hit the fan. Blamed for the death of Maggie Dorn, the mean bitch, Poor little Sara Cho was pulled, by her hair, out of the closet and roughly pushed into solitary confinement — there was hell to pay. The jail nurse did a quick check, the petechial hemorrhage in Maggie's eyes determined strangulation to be the cause of death.

Haggard never returned and that was a stumper. He had been there approximately five years and never missed a shift. In the video recordings, the guards and the warden saw, Haggard brought both women into the closet. Sara was taken for questioning. She told the warden more than a few times that she didn't remember. He figured it was the same bullshit story she came in with. Everyone, including the guards, knew what Mean Maggie did to her — tit-for-tat — they tried to pin the murder on her. Sara Cho, the young college escort, was a casualty of war.

No one knew what happened to Haggard, not even

Haggard. An investigation opened, if you want to call it that. But the answer to why he took the two women into the closet remained a mystery. In theory, he did it to let Sara get revenge on her tormentor, but it was just a theory. When he didn't show up the next day, a couple of his co-workers went to his house and found nothing. Everything was clean and put away. He had no family — with his mother and father dead and no siblings. There was no one to look out for him. He was another statistic in a long line of statistics.

***

Cil didn't know where he was going; he didn't care. All he knew was that he had to dump the car — he didn't want it to be found. He kept going east and before he knew it, he was in Nebraska — the welcome sign lit bright by the headlights. A little later, a sign appeared, Rapid City. For some reason, he thought of Mount Rushmore, so he drove north. Highways changed, but the road felt the same. As the change of the day approached, blushes of blue and yellow submerged and blended within the shimmering night sky. Cil silently observed the change through the glass — a new day would come. A little rest area in the middle of nowhere became home for the time being, Cil slept on the grass, by a picnic table, a hundred feet or so away from the bathrooms. He drifted into his dreams...

***

The haunting darkness touched every corner, making him feel uncomfortably alone. The soundless sea waves splashed upon each other and the bland cries of sea birds rang numb in his ear. The feeling of vertigo compelled him to step back, even though he couldn't see the edge — it was the same cliff. Odd as it was, no clouds milked the sky, no stars glittered. He let his mind wander into the dream. Cil knew his eyes were open, but he trusted nothing. He knew, in the dream, nothing could happen, so he stepped forward. He should have fallen into the water, weighed by sin and hate, but stood before the cave. The darkness stood still; the cave opening couldn't be discerned, but he walked in knowing there was a space. Inside, the air was dank and salty. He walked until an invisible wall forced him to stop; he knew he wasn't alone. The darkness crept upon him — he stood, petrified.

He remembered those eyes — those red eyes that tore right through his soul. His breathing was heavy; sweat formed on his upper lip. He saw a movement, but it could have been nothing. It was so dark. The brain senses and feels things; his eyes saw and his brain knew, so he waited. A whisper at first, gradually developing to a maddening screech — there were so many wings. A hunk of night came straight at him, it came so close that Cil could almost see its face — *was that a grin?* Little details were becoming apparent, he wanted to see what this thing was, but fear pulled him, until he...

***

He opened his eyes. It was morning and travelers were resting, getting soft drinks for the road. A pretty big dog, that just pissed on his leg, was sitting and staring at him. He was afraid to move, not wanting the animal to freak out, but his bladder forced him to sit up — the dog just sat and stared. When he creaked to a stand, a woman called,

"Roofus! Get over here! Leave that man alone!"

He stood up and met the woman's eyes. Seeing an apology, he smiled and waved. The friendly dog ran to its master. Cil made his way to the bathroom. After splashing water on his face, he was ready to get back on the road. It was a bland day, with few clouds in the sky. The air was different, compared to Colorado. He stood by Haggard's car for a few minutes, breathing in the freedom, when an old man, with two Pugs, walked by.

"How far am I from Mt. Rushmore," Cil asked.

"Hell, boy! You're almost there! Just keep on north, you'll be smelling the president's breath long before you know it."

Cil thanked the old guy and pulled out from the rest stop. Surly they would be looking for the car by now — he had to get another. He figured there would be a used-car lot somewhere in Rapid City, so he let his mind ease. He didn't know he had passed into South Dakota earlier that morning. It surprised him. Rapid City came up pretty quick. A few miles into the city, Cil found a used-car lot but he drove by it. He didn't have the paperwork to sell or trade the car — *best to get rid of it*. He drove around and found an abandoned slaughter house. He parked the car out back in the high grass.

He passed by folks he assumed were Native Americans. He had never seen one up close and didn't know for sure. He asked one of them how to get back on the road that lead into town. The man was friendly enough to give him directions. *I saw an Indian!* — He was fascinated and surprised. Cil noticed the guy was wearing jeans and a flannel shirt, though it was hot. *Hmm! I can change bodies right now and no one would find me*. He changed his mind — those people had it hard. There was a sliver of goodness in him after all. He used that to justify breathing in the air that should have been unavailable long ago. He walked back to the used-car lot, smiling.

There was an old dude whose skin looked like dried leather, smoking a cigarette by the front door. As soon as he saw Cil walking up, he dropped his smoke and stamped it out. Cil barely crossed two feet before the man walked quickly toward him.

"Whatcha lookin' for, stranger?"

The man took off his brown cowboy hat and wiped his

forehead.

"I just need a car." Cil said.

The man had kind eyes, like the kind a grandfather has while looking at his grandson who sat on his lap listening to an old story.

"Well, I just happen to have a few."

The old man looked at where Cil had walked from.

"You passing through?"

"Yea, the bus overheated. That thing stunk anyway. If I can buy a car for less than a grand, I'll be grateful."

The old man squinted, *if this fellow had a thousand dollars to spend, why was he taking the bus?* But he learned, long ago, that too many questions equaled to no used-car sales, so he bit his lip. To the right, a few beaters grew old over a patch of overgrown grass. Cil followed the salesman.

"I've got a thousand dollars to spend, not a hundred. I'm going to need something better than this."

Cil pointed to a Ford Fairlane that looked like it wanted to die in peace. The old man grinned and motioned Cil to follow. They walked to the back of the lot. There were more cars; a few looked better and a few looked worse. It was beginning to drizzle — a welcome reprieve from the heat.

"Take a look around, sunny. Ima get some keys."

The salesman went through the back door and came out a minute later with a chunk of keys. He walked over to another Ford, opened the driver's door and started the thing. It grumbled and wined, but came to, huffing out some non-regulated smoke the EPA loved to hate.

"That's normal for these old things." The old man said.

The smoke blanketed them like they were in some massive forest fire. Before Cil could sit, the car grumbled again and died, letting out one last puff. The salesman cussed loudly and picked through the keys,

"She just needs to warm up. Have a look at this one."

He walked over to a Toyota and tried that one — it was dead. He bounced around to other cars. Cil stayed by the

Toyota — *I should try another lot.*

"Got one! This, my friend, is the car for you. She ain't much to look at, but she's strong and will get to where yer goin'."

Cil walked over to where the old man was standing. The salesman was motioning his hand like he was one of those models on a game show. Cil looked it over; it didn't look that bad. The body was in relatively decent shape. The engine sounded as good as a thousand-dollar car should.

"This little lady came in a few months ago. She ain't got no AC, but other than that, she's ready to go."

"How much?" Cil asked.

"I'll let 'er go for, let's see, 800?"

"I'll give you 700 for it." Cil said.

The old man put his hand up and rubbed his face, acting like it was a tough sale, but 700 was a hell of a lot more than he paid for.

"You got yerself a new car, my friend. Let's get on inside and get the title squared, then you can be on your way."

CHAPTER TWENTY-SIX

In the isolated darkness, an innocent girl (sort of) was paying for the death of an inmate. Still no word from Haggard and the questions were piling up. Dirt like this didn't take long to make its way through a small population. Jail was no different. On a Wednesday, Tabitha, Cil's old cell-mate, finally spoke up. She told a guard, who told his supervisor, who then told the warden. The story was about as believable as Jack climbing a beanstalk, but it was all they had. The warden brought Tabitha into his office and heard the whole story. He tried hard not to throw this crazy bitch into solitary, but — there is always a but!

The next morning, the warden called the FBI and related to them what he knew. The main office called Denver, and Jacob Miller was back on the case. He took the next flight to Casper, and went straight to interview Tabitha. Her story rang the same bell the NY detective rang. This case was beginning to sound more like something from The X-Files. But he had to go with what he had —and that was next to nothing.

Miller watched the tapes from the jail and talked to Sara Cho. The poor girl had no idea how she got to Casper. She stuck with the story that she didn't remember killing the trucker. It was all Deja-vu to Miller; he had heard this story before. The impossible started to become possible, maybe, even probable — that disturbed him. After completing his work, he checked into a hotel room and tried to put it all together. Just like in Fort Collins, he spread out all the files on the bed — like a puzzle. He tried to put the pieces into place. But the one piece, the most important piece, was missing- how the hell was this happening? Modern technology rose to the occasion. He spent all night researching about reincarnation on his smart phone. Early in the morning, he called the police station and had an APB put out on the guard. It was silly, but Occam's Razor...

***

Cil spent the night in a fancy hotel close to Mt. Rushmore. It was time he spent the money he didn't work so hard to get. Seeing the monument would take time, and the day was almost done. After waking up and getting dressed, Cil ate the free continental breakfast offered, which consisted of bagels, sausage, and cereal. He got in his car and drove to the famous monument he waited so long to see. The parking lot was full, hundreds of people, from all over the world, were gawking at the huge stone structure carved out of the mountain. The carved stone structures were 60ft high — the workmanship was remarkable. Cil spent half the day there. He took some time to plot his next move, but came up with nothing except to drive. He headed south. Six minutes later, he got pulled over for speeding by the South Dakota State Patrol.

***

An hour before, a man found the car Cil stashed behind the abandoned slaughter house in Rapid City. The keys were on the driver's seat. He got in and took off. He was pulled over, roughly at the same time Cil was pulled over, and told the trooper he found the car. The trooper, who worked that particular stretch of the city, knew the guy and believed him, yet he ran the vehicle's VIN. The check came back. The car belonging to a Bill Haggard from Casper, Wyoming. He immediately saw the APB and called it in.

****

When Cil pulled over, the officer asked for his license, registration, and proof of insurance. Cil leaned and pulled the title from the glove compartment, and handed it to the officer. He told him he had just bought the thing.

"Your license too please." The officer asked.

Cil told the man he lost it at Mt. Rushmore.

"OK, wait here a second."

The officer went back to his patrol car and ran the information. The APB popped on the computer screen saying Bill Haggard was wanted by the FBI. The officer exited his vehicle and pulled out his weapon, aiming it at the car. He ordered Cil out and to lie face down on the ground. Cil didn't know about the APB, but knew that once the guard went missing, people would look for him — well! They found him. The thought of going back to jail didn't sound appealing; he knew what he had to do. He got out of the car and did what he was told. The officer, foolishly neglecting to call for back-up, slowly walked toward Cil and put his knee on Cil's back. While he was reaching for his handcuffs, Cil made his move, twisting to his right and knocking the gun out from the officer's hand. The officer tried to compensate, but Cil was bigger. He managed to get on top. Cil punched the man, then reached for the gun and put it in the officer's mouth — he fired.

It was late in the afternoon and traffic was minimal, but two cars did go by and he was seen — he saw them and they saw him. One of them was a woman with her two kids in the backseat. She looked at Cil, who looked at her through her windshield, Cil smiled. The other car had a single man and he was stunned while Cil took off. When the coast was clear, the man got out, saw the dead officer, and called 911. By the time back-up arrived, Cil was hauling ass toward Custer State Park, few miles south of the monument. Multiple jurisdictions were called in and a massive manhunt was on. Once Jacob Miller arrived in Rapid City, he sped to the scene — Cil Franklen ditched the car and ran.

CHAPTER TWENTY-SEVEN

He knew officers were swarming every nook and corner of Custer State Park, and for the first time, after many years, Cil was dead scared. He shouldn't have killed the cop, but if he didn't, he'll be on his way to jail — that could not happen. Within an hour, helicopters were flying over hunting for him. They had heat sensors and night vision, and were constantly in touch with the ground units. When Miller pulled the jacket that covered the dead officer, he saw the dollar bill and almost smiled, but couldn't — he was still a dead man and a dead cop. Now, Jacob Miller had the command. It was the biggest case of his life and there was no way on God's green earth he would screw that up. He screamed orders to various police departments out there and had the whole park wrapped up tight as an 80-year-old prostitute — *I've got you, you son of a bitch!*

But it wasn't that easy; the park was full of people, camping and hiking. Deep red lit the PIR, Passive Infrared sensor, in the helicopters. Technology didn't exist to isolate one man, so, the process would take a longtime. Maybe in future, technology would allow people to be found by DNA, but that was somewhere in a Phillip K. Dick book, not in Custer State Park. Police dogs dragged their officers while sniffing, walking, and checking people. Miller had already sent someone to Haggard's house in Casper to retrieve something the dogs could use to identify. Currently, all they had was the scent from the car. Miller hoped that would be enough. When the darkness finally overcame, tired officers trudged on through the park. No one was allowed in or out, without a serious check — it was a sticky, warm night.

Cil ran until he became breathless. He saw the helicopters, and there was only one way out. He had to find a single person, preferably a man, camping alone. He had to be quick, quicker than Haggard's old body would allow. He saw a campfire way off and walked toward it, wiping his sweat from his forehead — he calmed himself. Cil had a greater advantage over the situation since most of the folks in the park didn't know what was happening. When he got close, he noticed this campfire had too many people, so he skirted and continued walking. After a quarter of a mile south, another fire appeared, and he saw a man sitting by it. As he walked closer, the man looked up and saw him, but there was no look of suspicion: why would there be?

"Hey buddy, this is embarrassing, but do you have an extra roll of toilet paper? Mine got all wet, and wiping my ass with leaves won't do wonders for my hemorrhoids."

The man got up and rummaged through a bag hanging from a tree nearby. While he was doing that, Cil picked up a big log by the fire and brained him over the head. The man fell down unconscious. A light beamed down, a few hundred yards away, from a helicopter; it was moving fast. This particular campsite was in the middle of a sizable patch of trees, so the light would do little good, but the heat sensors... He wanted to wait until the aircraft flew by before he switched bodies. He laid down a few feet from the man and watched it fly by. From the air, it looked like two men sleeping. They were looking only for one man, so it might buy him some time, but he knew the police would be coming on foot soon. When the light moved off west, Cil got up and sat by the unconscious man. He began his incantations and in less than a minute, he switched successfully.

He gained conscious after thirty seconds, thanks to the log which did its job well. He opened his eyes and saw Haggard sitting a few feet away; the guard looked lost. Cil stood up, rubbing his head and Haggard looked at him as if he was coming out of a dream. It would be easy to let the guard take the rap, but, like most serial killers, Cil wanted to be known — Cil started liking the chase. It motivated him and gave him the rush that fueled his thirst. While Haggard was foggily trying to understand where he was, Cil walked behind and snapped his neck — the dead can't talk. Before he left, he tucked a dollar bill into Haggard's shirt and walked out, grabbing the hanging bag in the process.

***

A road cut through the park and within the hour, Cil was on it, walking toward east. It didn't take too long for him to come upon a roadblock. he was stopped by the police. The questioning was short; they had a picture of Haggard and this wasn't him. The two witnesses, who saw Cil kill the trooper, gave descriptions to the police — they matched Haggard remarkably well. After checking Cil out, they let him go. The helicopter made another pass by the campfire, where Cil killed the camper, but before, there were two men sleeping, now only one. The pilot was ordered to call in anything odd. While this wasn't exactly odd, he called it in anyway. Miller and a small contingency of officers made their way there. When they arrived, Miller screamed angrily — he knelt down and took the dollar bill from the camper's shirt; the man's neck had been broken. This is the point where he really started to believe. They had Haggard, but he was dead, and the one who killed him put the bill where he could see it. It's almost impossible for the mind to believe the impossible, but when nothing else makes sense... Miller radioed and inquired if anyone left the park. The four officers who let Cil go lied and told, "No." They didn't like some government suit guy telling them what to do and since the camper didn't match their description, they let him go.

They searched until daylight, interviewing everyone. Haggard's body was on its way to forensics, aiming to pick up a fingerprint or some other DNA. The camper Cil took over had caught a ride into the park, four days earlier. He had a bunch of other people's stuff on him, like hair and skin particles. The forensic team found a bunch of that stuff, but it got them nowhere. They had nothing to compare it to. At daybreak, the officers who trolled the park all night exchanged their duty with another. It wasn't until afternoon that Miller found out a man DID leave the park during the night — he went ballistic. He knew he had to come clean about his suspicions, so he called a conference and spilled the beans — no one believed him.

Cil was on his way east, picked up by four hunters whose truck was full of empty beer cans. Jacob Miller took over the police captain's office and had all his files spread out on the desk. He gave the crew his profile and told the whole story from the beginning. He didn't have a description of anyone to look for, and like before, had squat to go on. His only lead was the man who got away. After getting a description of him from the officers who screwed up, he put it out. Within minutes, Cil was in the crosshairs again, but he didn't know it.

Miller sat in the police station waiting. There was nothing he could do now, but hope. He knew the camper was on foot; he had all roads leading from the park covered, but he was too late. Either someone would find the camper walking, or... he didn't want to think of the other, but knew — the man had got away.

CHAPTER TWENTY-EIGHT

All the major news stations were broadcasting the story. Forget Gain, Bundy, Dahmer, the Zodiac, and that freak trailer park killer; The Dollar Bill Killer was becoming the most proficient serial killer of all time. There was no system for this type of monster; he killed whenever he wanted and whoever he wanted. The D.C. snipers scared people in D.C., Berkowitz scared people in New York City, and Cil Franklen scared people everywhere. At one point, Dahmer was killing one person a week, Cil wanted to up that ante — he had work to do.

He had the hunters drop him off in the town of Wall in Pennington County. A handful of miles south was The Badlands National Park. This barren place looked like it was out of Dante's Inferno, with peaks of rock jetting out into the hot air like devil's teeth. It was dry and grey, but held games for hunters. The Lakota Indians used it as a hunting ground a long time ago — it still had bounty. Cil walked south from Wall; it took two hours to get to the place. It was spooky.

The mid-day sun was working its way down west, but it was still hot. Cil figured this was the last place anyone would look for him — *it was a pretty damn good spot for hiding*. He had nowhere to go and no time to get there, so walking in whatever direction suited him; that was the plan du jour. Earlier, while he was seated in the hunter's truck, a sick and evil idea brewed in his head — he wanted to duplicate Mt. Rushmore with real people. They would be dead, of course, like the presidents, but it would be a skin monument, not a stone one. He thought about the four men, but changed his mind. They had more guns than teeth, and if he tried anything, he would be the dead one — he had to be patient.

Arteries of dirt roads wove their way all through the Badlands and some people were there. It would take some time to find some huddled down, but time was everlasting. Cil had no water, his thirst was getting stronger than his desire to kill. Surly, there would be rest areas in this sprawling hell, but would they have water? There was a rock uprising that looked like a shark's fin — he rested on the eastern side of it, needing shade and a break from walking. There he spent the night. It was peaceful, the stars looked like they were ten feet away, but the night brought sounds — sounds he had never heard before. In the bag he took, he found a can of beans and some beef jerky. The beans needed a can opener, and he didn't have one. The jerky looked good; he ate half of it and his thirst magnified, causing him to lament over eating the dried beef — sleep took over.

***

In the night, he woke. He didn't know what woke him until the second shot. Cil jumped and scanned the darkness — another shot echoed, followed by distant yells of excitement. Leaving the bag, he walked to where the sound came from. He saw a flickering light some distance away. As he got closer, he saw the four hunters who gave him a ride to Wall — he was getting lucky! He didn't believe in God; so, he thanked the stars, which winked at him. It would be too risky to roll into their camp while they were awake. He watched them from a small mound. They were drunk and throwing away the beer cans into the campfire. The shots he heard were them shooting into the air while dancing around the fire. They did that for almost three hours, and when the beer was gone, they passed out. The fire slowly died; it was the embers that offered a scant light — he waited.

He wanted to be sure that they were really out. he moved into the camp, stepping softly on the crusted dirt. Cil didn't know much about rifles and it would be disastrous for him to pick one up only to have one shot left in it. One of the hunters, the super skinny one, had a revolver in a holster around his waist. Cil baby-stepped over to him and gently took the gun from the leather case. The man turned in his sleep — Cil froze, but the man didn't wake up. Cil brought the revolver up and opened it, making sure there were at least four rounds left. It took a minute, he didn't know much about revolvers either, but saw the release. Experimentation usually brought rise to innovation — it worked. He took another minute to position himself in the middle of the four, then shot all four in the heart.

It was a lonely place in the Badlands. Even the creatures walked alone. Gunshots were heard all the time, but no one would come. Cil had time to make his monument; it was grizzly work. He only had a knife to cut the men in half, which would take some time — he did it in silence. When that finished, he dragged the lower halves of the bodies (sans legs) near the fire, which was smoldering. He needed the light, so he added some logs and waited until the fire lived again. Working in the dark, he dug the foundations on the hard, dry dirt to set the torsos in, but had problems with the innards spilling all over the place. The first torso from the larger man was put in the earth for George Washington. Using dirt to cake it in, he turned it slightly to face southeast. Then he took the skinny man and put him in. The hunters had brought water, but they left it alone, Cil drank from the canteens while spilling some on the dirt to make make-shift mud. The third guy was the ugly one, while the other wasn't that bad; he had to save the man with the beard for Lincoln. After sticking in the last two torsos, he caked them in with more water, put on the top halves in random order, and tweaked their heads to where he remembered they were supposed to face.

It took him over four hours. When he was done, he pulled a plug of Redman tobacco from the bag and spat into the fire. He added more wood and piled the leftover body parts on it — the smell was horrible, but he sat through it. Earlier, while he was preparing the bodies, he found the keys to the truck and he left everything else to burn. He watched the flesh burn like bacon, rippling and cooking in its own fat. By the turn of the light, most of the meat had been eaten by the fire, leaving the clean white bones to shine in the early sun. He stuck a dollar bill on a stick and planting it in front of his monument. He got in the truck and left — the fire simmering.

CHAPTER TWENTY-NINE

Jacob Miller was sleeping, at the desk, when the station suddenly erupted. A group of officers were standing a few feet away staring at him — they looked horrified. The chief was sitting at the edge of the table a few feet away. He turned around and met Miller's eyes; his own red and stressed out. He motioned the FBI man to come over.

"Something happened? What is it?" Miller asked.

"This is fucked up and you won't believe it. Hell, I didn't believe it until I saw it and even then, I... I've never seen shit like this."

The chief told Miller to follow him. They went to the waiting chopper and flew to the crime scene. When they arrived, the bird landed fifty yards from the camp so as not to spew dust and dirt all over. They walked to the mess that used to be living human beings. The police chief stopped and told Miller to go ahead on his own; he didn't want to see it again, so soon. There were forensic people dusting and going over every inch on the campsite. When Miller walked up, they stopped and looked at the chief, who nodded at them to take a break — Miller stood alone.

He, of course, had seen something like this, in Fort Collins, Colorado, with two homeless men splayed like

Vlad the Impaler's victims, but it didn't lessen the horror. The afternoon sun was beating down, burning the pale, bloodless bodies. The fire had long since played its tune and the bones left laid like a grave in a Bosnian genocide hole — Miller was overwhelmed. There were sick people out there. He learned about them at the academy, through pictures, but this was stinking right in front of him. *Why did he do like this?* — for a moment, only just a moment, he questioned it all. Then he called the crime scene team over.

"Tell me all that you know."

The woman in charge, a pretty woman in her 40s, took a breath and explained what she saw. They were shot first, in their hearts; they were instantly fatal. The knife, she pointed at with a number card next to it, was what cut the men in half. She went on to explain the next steps, and when she was done, she waved her hands over the "monument" — that was the finished product.

"It definitely took some time." She said.

"How were they discovered?" Miller asked.

"The chief said a hunter came across them this morning. He's right over there. They've been dead for maybe 10-to-12 hours. Is this the same man you've been looking for?"

Miller looked at the dollar bill flying from the stick and nodded.

"Yes."

She followed Miller's gaze.

"You have to get this guy."

Miller nodded again.

He stayed there for over an hour, just staring at the scene; he was trying to see through the mind of the killer, but was having a hard time doing it.. Without saying a word, he walked back to the chopper and waited for it to take off back to the station, but changed his mind. He went back to the chief, who was still watching from a distance.

"Those men drove here. Did we know that they drove?" Miller asked.

The chief paused, like it was something that he hadn't thought of — then his eyes widened.

"No, but you're right."

He looked around and called for one of his deputies to come over.

"Was there a vehicle here when you got here?"

"No, sir."

The deputy himself looked around and caught the drift.

"I'm on it," he said and walked away.

***

Cil was driving. He drove through the night passing every light that flickered at him. The cool air blowing in, from the open window, freed him, like he was flying on a magical horse from the toils of the insane world which he was a part of. His clothes were dirty and bloody, but he felt fine — "swell" as Clint Eastwood would say. He was on Interstate 90 going east, just passing Belvidere. He had slept all day in the truck, on a dirt road, many miles back. He didn't know where he was going — he didn't care.

Bad dreams didn't come when he slept earlier. Maybe because he was in the truck or it just wasn't time, but he was ok with that. The truck was his spaceship and the road his space. He drove with a grin only a madman could have. He would push on to the Missouri River and clean himself there, reenacting what demented soldiers did after killing Indians more than a hundred years ago. The river held a lot of blood and nightmares, but it flowed clean today.

Jacob Miller didn't have any information, yet he assumed that the son of a bitch who took the vehicle would use the interstate to get across the country. He made a call to Sioux Falls and had them dispatch units to the highway. Miller was tired, and sleep was becoming a luxury; he wanted this guy.

The truck Cil had been driving had a CB radio which he turned on — it was on channel 19. Truckers were chatting away about women, food, politics, and the killer on the loose; Cil listened attentively. Most of the truckers wanted a piece of him, and if they saw him, it would be highway justice. One of the voices said, he wanted to "skin the piece of shit alive," which made Cil swallow his salvia. His motivation to get to the Missouri was increasing; he had to clean the blood off. He hadn't eaten a whole meal in two days, except for jerky, and his stomach was rumbling.

When he finally got there, he drove through a state highway named, 47, branching south, going 8 miles before the great river became visible. He stopped, took all his clothes off, and jumped in. The White River inked off to the west and it was less rigid than the Missouri. He stayed in the water until his skin oiled and became pruney, then he washed his clothes to the best he could and hung them out to dry. It was a pleasant night; he propped himself against a rock and listened to the water. Before he knew it, he drifted off into his dreams

Miller flew to Sioux Falls at 8:14 a.m. The chopper wasn't available, so he took one of those puddle jumpers. The small plane landed at 9:36 a.m. He met a deputy who immediately took him to the station. When he walked in, he asked for an update on the night's happenings — there was none. The chief met Miller in his office, they hashed out a plan.

"I'm pretty sure he's going to come through here. That's what he does; he stays at populated areas so he can do his work. I don't know where he is now, and trust me, that pisses me off, but he'll come through here."

The chief pulled out a pack of cigarettes and offered Miller one.

"Don't you think, if he sees all the men on the road, he'll divert and go somewhere else?" The chief asked Miller.

"Yea, I've been thinking about that. Maybe we should pull the marked cars off and have civilian vehicles staked out."

There was a pause while the chief looked at the FBI man for a few seconds.

"Listen, there are some weird rumors going around about this guy changing bodies. Yesterday, when you contacted us, I was willing to go along, but now I need more information. Who the hell is this guy? Yea, I've heard about him — everyone has. He's been cutting down people from New York to Colorado and I know what he did to the hunters in the Badlands. It's this body changing that I don't get. Are we talking about *Invasion of the body snatchers* kind of shit here?"

Miller sighed — he was tired of explaining, tired of trying to explain what he didn't understand. He asked the chief to close the office door. Most of the officers outside had heard about it already, but only one believed it; a man from New Orleans. When Miller was done, the chief called in that man and shut the door.

"This is Denzel Foshet, he's from New Orleans. He might have some insight on this whole mess."

The chief nodded to his deputy. It was obvious, the man had something to say. He put his hand out and shook Miller's — they sat down.

"From where I'm from, people believe in spirits who can possess other people. Now, I'm a Christian and I don't run with those folks, but some in my family do. I've seen some weird shit, people doing weird shit, but I always chalked it to drugs and mind control. But it does exist, at least in the minds of those who believe."

"How? How does it happen?" Miller asked.

"I left that area long ago, mostly because of that. That's why I'm here, instead of there. Like I said, I don't believe in black magic. But you've seen those exorcist movies, right? Well, that's how. Sometimes it's the devil and sometimes it's someone else, and when they do their rituals with dead chickens and all that, people change. I don't know how exactly, but I've seen people walking around like zombies after being thought dead. Is this "Dollar Bill Killer" from Louisiana?"

"No, he's from New York." Miller said.

"*Hmmmm,* that's odd. Listen! I don't know much about it. I told the chief here what I've seen and he thinks I'm an expert on the whole thing, but I'm not. When I was old enough to get the hell out of that part of the world, I did — that's it. I don't know what else to tell you, sir."

"Where do YOU think he will go next?" Miller asked the deputy.

It was good for morale to bring others into the fray, and plus, this guy might actually be right.

"If I had to guess, and that is exactly what I'm doing, I figure he'll come through here. How smart is this guy — I mean, he's gotta be pretty quick to evade you, but if he's into black magic and changing bodies, well, I don't know..."

"He's getting arrogant. The dollar bills he leaves shows that he thinks he's smarter than us. Thanks for your insight deputy! We better get back to the highway."

Miller crushed out his fifth cigarette and left the office. He took a car and drove out of Sioux Falls by himself.

***

It was nearly noon. Cil was about to enter the gauntlet. The chief came up with nothing on the vehicle, but he expected that. Everything at the crime scene had been burned, except for the four men. It would take more time to run a check on them. Cil saw the multitude of police cars lining the eastbound side of highway 90. He kept going.

Maybe four or five miles into the gauntlet, there was a checkpoint. They didn't know what to look for, the person or the vehicle, so they just looked for anything suspicious. When Cil came to the stop, he was asked a few questions and let go. There was a van in front of him that had been pulled to the side of the highway, it contained twelve illegal immigrants from Mexico. When the police were busy with that, Cil slipped through — he almost crapped his pants. He was so relieved that his arrogance grew stronger. He continued heading toward south, on Highway 29. After a few miles, he entered Sioux Falls. He stopped at the first gas station and found out the location of the police station, bought a Mountain Dew, and drove to the lion's den — they would never expect this!

CHAPTER THIRTY

Miller was fidgeting with his cell phone in the borrowed police car — it was hot. The sweat dripped from his face down to his already wet shirt. Perhaps his nerves added to the heat. He sipped on his second bottle of Gatorade and watched the sun etch down the western sky. Highway 90 crossed with highway 29 back about two miles. He had heard nothing positive. Three times he checked the gauntlet and came back with nothing. He knew it was a bad idea to have the marked cars lined up — maybe the fucker saw them and took another route. His phone slipped from his sweaty hands, it dropped down on the floorboard — he left it there. With nothing to play with, his mind relaxed enough to shut down a little, he fell asleep. It was a rugged sleep which only lasted for 17 minutes — his phone rang — he didn't hear it.

The loud cackle from the police radio spit into the hot car waking Miller up. Disoriented, he reached down to get his cell and answered. The radio spit again, his mind understood the second time.

"Yea, Miller here."

He threw the cell phone on the passenger seat and wiped his face with his left hand.

"Miller? Where are you? We've been calling your cell."

The police chief's voice was a reminder of the real world.

"I slipped off for a minute. What's up?"

"There's a letter here for you. Someone just brought it in, said it was important."

"Who?"

"Don't know, just some guy. He left it at the front, one of my men brought it to me. Hold on a second, 'Hey Johnson, who brought it in?'"

A few seconds elapsed. Miller didn't hear the response, then...

"He said, the man said, 'he was a friend of yours'. Do we have two feds here?"

"Not that I know of. They would have told me another was coming. Can you open it and read it to me?"

Miller's shirt was sticky and wet; he was getting uncomfortable.

"Aren't you coming in?" The chief asked.

"Not just yet. Open it and read it to me."

"All right, hold on."

The faint sound of paper ripping and a long pause.

"Is this a fucking joke?"

"What? What are you talking about?"

"It's a dollar bill."

The chief said something in the background Miller couldn't understand. Then the sound of the phone being placed on the desk and movement.

"Chief?"

Silence.

"CHIEF?"

"Yea, I'm back. We're pulling the video now. Pretty fucking brazen, don't you think? Is this guy toying with us?"

Miller was already speeding to the station. He heard the last transmission, but didn't respond. *Is this bastard this arrogant?* — It takes a lot of balls to walk into a police station, where everyone in the country is looking for you, and leave a message like that. He imagined how it happened — how the man walked into the station. How he handed the envelope to the deputy, at the front desk. How he walked out. Was he smiling? Did he look at a camera? Miller took the last left to the brick building and ran inside. Hidden, watching closely, Cil Franklen saw the FBI man almost drive the car onto the grass — he was indeed smiling. When Miller disappeared into the structure, Cil drove away, heading north of downtown. Sioux Falls was a nice place, with not so many seedy areas. The worst seedy area was Disney Land compared to the best seedy areas of other major cities. The area north of downtown fit that bill. Cil passed 9th and Phillips, and drove a tad farther. He parked the truck, and blended in with the grain. Within minutes, he found his next victim.

***

Miller was handed the envelope as soon as he entered the chief's office. He took it with a tissue and put it into a plastic bag while ordering prints to be taken. This wasn't the world in the CSI TV show, where prints came back within the hour. Even if they did, it would be hard to find one man in a city with almost 155,000 people. Knock out about half for the female population, and that still left too many for a police department of around 300, *what if this prick changed bodies again?*

Miller noted the time by watching the video. Twenty-two minutes passed between the time the "Dollar Bill Killer" dropped off the envelope and Miller entered the police building. Miller took into account how fast traffic moved downtown between driving and walking. He came up with a square that he ordered blocked off. As a side note, he thought about the city bus system. He wanted it tight. Every officer was pulled off from whatever he/she was doing and re-assigned to the pinch. The son of a bitch had to be close and Miller wanted to make sure he didn't slip out this time. As hundreds of officers set up around the new trap zone, Cil Franklen was brushing off the dirt from his face. He had just taken on a homeless man, and the old body — that of the camper — was snuffed out with a plastic bag. Before Cil left the area, behind the Italian restaurant, he wedged a dollar bill into the cracks of the brick building. He then walked around the building and sat in front of the thrift store next to the restaurant with a discarded Slushy cup, waiting for the show to begin.

CHAPTER THIRTY-ONE

Jacob Miller drove downtown and stopped by a coffee shop. He was in the trap zone and kept the volume of his radio at a peak level. The bulk of Sioux Fall's police force slowly squeezed in. Even an out of place baseball cap was looked at carefully. There were two officers in the area: one, a mean old bastard, who handed out speeding tickets like they were free snow cones; the other, a rookie, who had the reputation of getting more tail than any other officer. They walked around the shops and eateries in the neighborhood of the Italian restaurant. The rookie split off and walked down the side street behind the restaurant. When he neared the dumpster, he stopped and lit up a cigarette. His partner hated smoking; so, he couldn't do it near him. As his smoke whisked away into the blue sky, he saw the tail of a dollar bill flapping in between the bricks. Alarmed, he immediately called his partner, who came running down the side street as fast as his overlapping hanging belly allow. The veteran officer got close to the bill, but didn't touch it. He radioed Miller, who was two blocks away. Miller came running. Dozens of townspeople, who were in the vicinity, stopped and gawked; it wasn't every day that they got to see a real FBI agent. Within twenty minutes, the crime scene folks arrived and dusted the area.

Miller shared a smoke with the rookie while he was getting the low-down on how the officer found the bill. His mind folded — something didn't fit — *why was there a dollar bill here?* It took him over an hour to figure it out.

"Did anyone check the dumpster?"

The two officers looked at each other and nodded their heads. The crime scene people were busy, and they too nodded their heads. Miller dropped his cigarette, crushed it, and went to the dumpster. As soon as he opened the lid, he saw the body.

"Everybody Stop, JUST STOP! We've been here for FUCKING hours and nobody, nobody thought to check the dumpster?"

He was pissed, but more at himself; he was partly at fault for not checking. The coroner was called and the body examined. It was determined that the man died from asphyxiation; a plastic bag stuck in the man's mouth. The body was loaded into the ambulance that rolled up without lights or sirens. Miller yelled and had the chief tighten the grip.

"He's in the city somewhere."

The area cleared; Miller was the only one left. He walked around the building and stood by the street, staring at the sky. There was a homeless man sitting in his filth a few feet back, against the wall.

"Did you see anyone going down there?"

He pointed down the side street.

"Got any change?" The homeless man asked.

"Anyone? Did you see anyone? Anything strange?"

"Got any change?" The man asked again.

"No, I haven't got any change. Get a fucking job, or do something for society, but answer my question, asshole."

He knew he shouldn't be taking to him like that; it wasn't like him, but his nerves got the best of him and the lack of sleep contributed. He stood there, about to kick the man in the head, but the man just looked at him and held the cup.

"I'm hungry."

Miller resisted the urge to kick him. He reached into his pocket, pulled out a five-dollar bill and threw it at the poor guy.

"You smell like shit" — and walked away.

Cil leaned forward and picked up the money. He carefully folded it and put it into his right front pocket; this he would save for something special. He sat there throughout the day. When the darkness began setting in, he got up, stretched, and casually strolled into the night.

***

Morning came quick for Miller; he managed an hour of sleep, if you could call it that. Being frantic throughout the night, he and the officers combed the square area trying to squeeze their prey, but nothing came of it. He started biting his nails again, they were skimmed deep into the flesh. He thought he had him, but he couldn't understand how the bastard slipped through. It bothered him all night, even in his thin sleep. The idea of Occam's Razor shot up and the only thing he could think about was the guy being still there. If this man kept changing bodies, which became a fact, he could have walked right by the son of a bitch without knowing. That was the part that chapped his ass more than anything. If there was a possibility for a movie like Jurassic Park to become a reality, thanks to DNA, a man changing bodies by some sort of reincarnation seemed about right as rain — *what the hell was this world coming to?*

He remembered, as a child, the only thing they had to listen to music on-the-go was a Walkman. It took cassette tapes which were in the size of a book. Now, they had iPods and MP3 players as small as a box of matches that held thousands of songs. Cell phones were unheard of back then, but by now everyone had one. There were guns that could fire hundreds of rounds of ammo in a split second and missiles that could wipe out whole cities. With the evil in the world, he picked one of the jobs to deal with it. How many nights were spent, when his eyelids felt like iron, thinking about if he had stayed home and played football. But in those nights, he knew he was doing exactly what he was supposed to do.

After a breakfast of orange juice and a power bar, he canvassed the area around the restaurant asking if they saw anyone strange or different — one person came up repeatedly, the homeless man. A lot of people saw him sitting with his cup, but nobody had ever seen him before. He rewound his memory back to the day before and went over the conversation. In that playback, he saw the homeless man almost grinning. He spoke to a woman who walked her dog across the street. She told him the man never got up. She walked her dog three times, and he was in the exact the same spot. She was a kind woman, but the man was a stranger — stranger spelled danger — she didn't go over to him.

Miller rounded the corner and went to the spot where the homeless man once sat. It was an evenly sunny day and the building's shadow spread across the sidewalk. He stood, looking across the street for a minute or two, then sat down himself. The concrete felt cool under his slacks; he let his mind wander. The sun was behind him, as he leaned against the brick wall, time moved on. The shadow receded closer and closer up his legs until half his body was sinking by the light. When the light reached his chest, he stood up, causing his cell phone to drop from its case. When he reached down to pick it up, he saw that something had been scratched onto the cement. The etchings were shallow, but readable:

MILLER!

The FBI man pounced back as if he was just been bitten. He was petrified for fully ten minutes, and cursed his stupidity for missing the obvious. That son of a bitch was there the whole fucking time — he even talked to him! This guy had balls. Miller pulled his cell phone, but thought against it, he slipped it back. Clouds were moving, but he was frozen. The plans he made: the traps, the squeezing, the following — all for nothing. He wondered if he was being watched; his mind was spinning without answers — he didn't know what to do.

CHAPTER THIRTY-TWO

After Cil walked by his hunter, he waited half a block away before turning around. The FBI man was standing, facing up to the sky. His eyes were closed, tears worked their way down; it was the look of failure. It moved Cil to a small degree; he knew what it felt like. The boy stopped, took out a pencil from his backpack, and wrote on something. He went up to the man standing outside the barber shop and asked him to give it to the man down the street. He disappeared around the corner. The barber looked at the five-dollar bill, but didn't see the note on it. He started to walk to the man down the street, but the phone rang. Two hours later, he remembered and made his way to the police station. Miller was at his temporary desk, face burried in his hands. The barber knew most of the folks there, so they allowed him to walk in. Miller looked up; the barber handed him the five-dollar bill. He explained that a boy had asked him to give it to him.

"Maybe you dropped it." The barber said and walked out.

Miller put the bill on the desk and saw the note: *Ever tried. Ever failed. No matter. Try again. Fail again. Fail better.*

He grabbed the bill and crumbled it up in his fists. The

writing was a quote from the playwright, Samuel Beckett —
he didn't know that, he didn't care. The chief walked by and
saw Miller rolling the crumbled ball.

"Money coming that easy for ya? They must be paying
you pretty well, eh?"

The chief sat down on the chair, next to the desk. Miller
slid the ball over to him.

"Read it."

The chief shrugged his shoulders and opened the mess
up; it was on the opposite side.

"Yea, it's a five-dollar bill. So?"

"Turn it over, Einstein."

The head of the police department didn't like that.

"Listen, man! You're a stranger here. We didn't ask you
to come, so you can drop that bullshit sarcasm right now."

"Just turn the thing over and read it, please!"

Miller's mind was soup and the chief's backlash didn't
bother him. The chief did as he was asked and saw the note.

"It's a quote."

"Yea."

"I've read this before – Samuel Beckett, an Irish writer.
Good stuff! Am I missing something here?"

"He was there the whole time. Remember that homeless
guy? Well, it was him. The man that just left gave it to me."

"The Barber? Why?"

"A boy gave it to him to give it to me. A fucking boy! I'll
give you two guesses who that boy was?"

"What boy? I didn't see any boy. Listen! You're being
kind of coy. Can you give me a little more information
here?"

Miller sighed.

"The homeless man and the boy were the same person —
the man we're after. He's playing with us, and he's
winning."

"Wait a minute! Are you telling me that this guy changed
from a homeless man into a boy, and gave the barber a five-

dollar bill with a note on it and just walked away?"

"I gave the money to him first."

"Huh?"

"When we wrapped up the other day, I walked by the homeless man, and gave him five bucks. I talked to him — told him that he smelled like shit. My God! He must be laughing his ass off right now."

The chief was thinking.

"Well, if that's true, there's a homeless man walking around town, right now, who doesn't know where he is, right?"

He paused.

"I mean, you said this guy changes bodies — what happens to the bodies that he leaves behind? Logically, as if logic worked here, the body that is left behind — the man, shouldn't know what happened. All the stuff gets transferred to the new body; in this case, the boy. And that brings about a new shit storm. Someone's son is no longer their son."

He paused, again.

"Am I anywhere close?"

"As close as I am, chief. And that's not very close."

"Then why are you sitting here, with your face buried in your hands. Let's get out and find that prick."

"He would have changed by now. I don't even know where to start."

"We'll start by finding the boy and the homeless man. This town isn't that big — someone will pass by them, sometime today."

At that, the chief walked over to the front desk and had the deputy put APBs on the two.

"Come on, G-Man. Let's get going!"

***

Cil had changed bodies; he was now a woman. He only used the boy for a single purpose — to screw with Miller.

He never wanted to hurt a kid. When he morphed out of the boy, the woman he became walked the boy to where he found him, and left him with plenty of mothers, in the park, to take care of the rest. Now, he sat in a bar, drinking scotch and water, and chain-smoking shitty cigarettes.

After he was totally drunk, he wobbled down to the bus station and found out that the next bus was leaving to Chicago. He bought a ticket. Cil sat on the cheap seats, at the station, for two hours and eleven minutes navigating a slippery sleep. When the bus came, Cil was ready to go.

As far as traveling goes, buses suck, but he had no other option; he didn't want any traces. Going by bus was different- if you paid cash, you didn't have to show an id. It was a rainy night, few people boarded in Sioux Falls. He had the two seats to himself. Before long, the alcohol got to him. He drifted into a sugary sleep: the kind where nothing is comfortable and the mind goes a little haywire. Thoughts slipped in and out, and when he woke up, twenty minutes later, the loaf of bread his mind was baking was rising. He massaged it until the idea became a plan. He should have done it earlier, but that carried a high risk. He turned on his cell phone attracting a dirty look from a passenger, across the row. He looked for small towns with less people nearby. When he found one, he set the alarm clock, figuring the miles into minutes — he slipped into sleep once again.

PART THREE

CHAPTER THIRTY-THREE

The bus followed highway 90, leaving South Dakota behind. He was now in Minnesota — the North Star State, where Lake Superior splashed onto the city of Duluth, in the east, and the sprawling country of Canada, bordered the state to the north. The ride was smooth. When the alarm went off, Cil woke up still groggy. He walked up the aisle toward the driver and asked if he could be let off in the town called King's Crossing —it was half hour from the city of Albert Lea, close to highway 35, leading north to Minneapolis.

"I'm not scheduled to stop there, ma'am." The driver said.

Cil reached into his money belt, pulled out a hundred-dollar bill, and handed it to the driver.

"I'd appreciate it if you stopped," he said.

The driver looked at the bill for a second, then took it and put it in his front pocket. He just doubled his pay for the night and one extra stop wouldn't screw up the schedule that much.

"I can drop you off on the side of the road. I have a schedule to keep and can't drive around looking for the bus stops."

"That's fine." Cil replied, standing.

A few minutes later, they entered the small town of King's Crossing. The driver stopped the bus near a McDonalds; Cil walked out excited.

After the bus was out of sight, Cil went to McDonalds and sat on one of the benches, near the entrance. It was forty-three minutes to five and the place would open soon. It was quiet, and Cil just watched the night turn into day. When the doors opened at five, he went in and ordered breakfast, with a large cup of coffee. McDonalds had come a long way and their coffee was pretty good. When he was done filling his belly, he nursed the coffee with his thoughts and worked on his idea. It was fresh and original; he was excited about it. The population of the town was 982 — he figured it wouldn't be that hard.

As more and more people poured in to the restaurant, Cil decided to leave. It wouldn't be too hard to find the Sherriff's office, when the whole town's population could fit into a college basketball auditorium. He left smiling, thinking he had hit the jackpot of malevolent ideas. The plan was simple, as simple as it goes. He would take over the Sherriff, then take over the town, by killing each inhabitant one-by-one. It would take a while, but he had it, time was just a blanket laid out for a killing spree.

Sherriff!

The word vibrated in his noodle for a while, who would ever guess? Now, Cil had watched his share of small-town TV shows, like *The Andy Griffith Show*. He figured most of the town folks knew each other. Having the Sherriff stop by for a personal visit wouldn't seem too odd, but he had some watching to do; he couldn't just waltz into the station. No matter! The money belt was beginning to wear on him, and had little use for it anymore. This would be the last stop for a while and money seemed redundant. It was time for him to settle down.

As he left McDonalds, a woman with a horde of kids

walked by. He nonchalantly asked where the Sherriff's office was. She pointed down the street to the left, and said,

"There are only two stoplights in this town, one intersects a railroad crossing. The Sherriff's office is next to that."

Cil ambled over.

***

It was early morning and shops were opening up. Across the street from the Sherriff was an old steam engine — it used to be a hotdog joint, long after the beast retired. Cil sat on the metal bumper and waited until life entered the office across the street. A little before seven, a beat-up Ford truck rolled in and a large man stepped out, stretching his worn-out body. He wore jeans and a brown, button up, short sleeve shirt with the town's name on it. On his hip was a big gun, not the pussy .38 many cops used, but a "Dirty Harry." The man had an eagle tattoo on his left forearm, which was twice the size of a normal man's. He had a gut, but wasn't fat – just large. Before he was Sherriff, and Vietnam, he worked on the railroads; he was the kind of man who could pick up a railroad tie and sling it around like a baby — Cil began to re-think his plan.

Perhaps a deputy! That might do, but the plan was the same. He watched a little longer. Soon after the Sherriff pulled up, a nervous, little man drove up in an older model Nissan pickup truck; it was tree frog green and ugly as hell. He got out of the vehicle and checked himself in the driver's side window, primping his brown uniform like a new Marine recruit. When he found himself fit enough, he walked into the building just as nervous as he arrived. Cil had his man.

He got up and went inside the section of the train that had last ran along the beautiful countryside, long ago. Graffiti trashed the metal walls and beer cans littered the floor. There was a couch along the northern wall which looked relatively fresh, so he sat on it. A few spiders felt the intrusion and headed out for quiet pastures. Rays of sunlight sought an entrance through a small window to spring its light. The light beams magnified the dust particles flying around. The warmth made him sleepy, he drifted off.

When he saw the light, he was amazed. It was phenomenal but scary, since it was dark. He squinted his eyes to see the pinch of light dissolve — darkness set in. He was in the cave; he didn't want to be there, but dreams went that way. This time, he didn't do the whole journey thing, he was just there. But in that quick instant, he saw bodies stuck in and out of the dirt and rock. It resembled the underground tunnel graves that were all over Europe — the victory of the Bubonic Plague. Skulls rested here and there, some with the frame and some without. He didn't smell anything, but there was an odor — a stale musty smell that aged a century. He picked up one of the skulls by the empty eye sockets and rolled it down the cave. *Ha! That's interestingly funny*, but it came back, this time with flesh and hair, and eyes that stared straight at him. It was dark, he caught a glimpse of a smile, a haunting smile that ended with a scream.

He woke.

***

The sunset made orange brush strokes across the sky and the absolute silence was wonderful. He was sweating, his pink shirt was wet from the neck down. Being a woman made his job easier. Since he had nowhere else to go, he stayed there. The night brought lower temperatures and a slight breeze blew through the steel monster. He stayed up watching the stars for a while, but gradually, boredom consumed him. It was a good time to explore the town; the night offered anonymity. He walked across the street to the sheriff's building. It was dark except for a dim light — only a deputy pulled the graveyard shift inside. He wanted to check it out, but that would be too risky. He was sure that the man he wanted was home, asleep. He walked down the main street and followed it to the end of town, which took 30 minutes. The other stoplight was by a home repair store, next to a school, followed by a convenient store, and McDonalds. That was the whole town, except for the houses and mobile homes that veined down the side streets. All around, there were small shops offering used furniture and oddities: Oh, and one diner — *how the hell did they pay for the cops here*?

When he arrived back to his temporary home, the old steam engine, he climbed on top and laid down. It was amazing how ancient people navigated the world by looking at the stars. Cil didn't sleep that night; he wondered about the world and his part in it. His mark wasn't made, yet — he had much to do.

CHAPTER THIRTY-FOUR

Jacob Miller and the sheriff ripped through town looking for the homeless man. They found him by the same dumpster from before. Now, Miller knew the game he was going to face, so he was prepared. The man slumped down between the dumpster and the building knew nothing, but every horse had to be checked. The sheriff stood by with his hand on his weapon while Miller questioned the man. Two bottles of vodka were lying close by. One was empty, and the other was still in the man's hand – a mouthful still left. The man could barely talk, they left without any information.

"I figured that. Now, the boy." Miller said.

"I know most of the folks in town, so finding the kid won't be that difficult. What did he look like?"

The sheriff lit up a cigarette and held out the pack for the FBI man. He lit one up. Miller described the boy and what he was wearing.

"Sounds like Sue Ellen's boy. She has a couple of daughters too. Come on, they don't live that far from here."

When they arrived at Sue Ellen's house, the boy was outside playing with those intricate Transformer toys. Miller recognized him right away. The sheriff knocked on the door and talked to the mother while Miller sat down on the grass next to the kid. When Sue Ellen saw that, she freaked out and ran outside, not knowing who Miller was. A short explanation fixed that and the sheriff took her back inside. Telling her the truth was out of the question. He told her Jason might have seen something at the park.

Miller waited until the boy looked up before he started questioning. First, he asked him his name, and then told who he was — the kid's eyes widened.

"A real-life FBI agent? Do you have one of those cool badges?"

Miller reached into his back pocket, pulled the badge out, and handed it to the boy.

"It's heavy." Jason said.

"That's because it's real. The fake ones are plastic. Can I ask you some questions?"

"OK." Jason said

He went back to play with his toys. Miller watched as a plane turned into a robot.

"We didn't have those when I was your age. What is that one called?"

"Optimus Prime. He's a good guy. See! He can turn into a plane. The other ones can turn into other things, like trucks."

"Wow! That's cool. Do you remember giving me a five-dollar bill the other day?"

Jason looked up.

"Huh? I gave you money?"

"Well! No, but you gave it to someone else to give it to me. Don't you remember that?"

"Uh-uh. My mom gave me ten dollars last week because I did good on my report card, but I bought a Transformer with it. Why did I give you money?"

Miller decided against questioning further; it was obvious, the boy knew nothing. He probably didn't even remember being blacked out.

"Maybe it was someone else. What grades did you get?"

"Four As and one C. I'm not good in math. Mom says she will give me more money if I do more stuff around the house."

"Tell you what, Jason. I'll match what your mom gave you."

Miller took out his wallet and pulled a ten-dollar bill and gave it to the boy.

"Buy another good guy."

He stood up and walked back to the car. The sheriff came out soon after. As they were driving back to the station, a call came through the radio about a woman missing — the two men looked at each other.

***

Early in the morning, Cil jumped down from the top and went to the dirty couch. Thoughts were like swarms of locusts, and when they came in, they disrupted everything. He tried to file all of the madness into neat, little stacks, but it was too much. He woke up around noon to the sound of laughing across the street. The new deputy was just pranked, his truck was wrapped in plastic, all the way around. The sheriff and his wife, a portly woman in her 50s, filmed the reaction with their phones. The deputy tried to cut away all the plastic. He didn't take it so well, and that made the whole affair funnier. Cil watched as the grumpy deputy walked into the station. He plotted his way into the man's body. After two hours, the deputy had an errand to run by the diner, a mile away from the station. Cil watched the man, who left and came back, grumpier than before.

Night fell across the small town of King's Crossing. The shift change took place at the sheriff's station at 9:00 p.m. The deputy left first, driving away in a police car while the sheriff left in his truck. Everyone knew that truck and everyone knew to whom it belonged. Cil didn't see the relief person come in. He wondered if anyone was in the building at all. It didn't matter anyway. Cil had to find out where the deputy lived. He couldn't run fast enough to follow the police car down the road. When the street lights came on, he began to make his way down the main street. He had to divert down all those side streets to find the police car. When he got to the diner, the lights shut off and two women came out carrying Styrofoam boxes with their dinner. They got into the same car, turned left on the main road, and went down until the tail lights disappeared.

It was about half mile to the school and a dirt road led off to the right. Cil took that and followed it as it wormed around in a semi-circle, ending on the other side of the convenient store. Across the street, another dirt road took off from the McDonalds and went down a few hundred feet; he was back where he started. Seeing nothing, he made his way back down the road. Highway traffic pounded highway pavement; the sound disturbed him. He had walked half across the football field before he saw the police car — it was parked outside a double wide trailer. He stopped and looked for a light — there was a flicker.

Walking close to a cop's house, late at night, was dangerous. Neighbors in small towns like this were close and they talked. He crept closer, trying to stay in the darkness. The little yard had a little fence with a little gate — he wouldn't dare open that, so he skirted the south side of the trailer and looked in through the living room window. The deputy was watching TV in a recliner; luckily, his back was to the window. Cil nudged his head close to the glass and looked in carefully, trying not to show himself. Cil figured the man lived alone. After watching the deputy for a minute or two, Cil distanced himself from the window and walked away. He had to come another day, but now, he knew where he lived.

The next morning, Cil woke up itchy; he hadn't killed in a while, and the urge was building in him. He had to take the deputy tonight! Throughout the day, he stared at the metal walls of the old steam engine. His mind was full; there was always something lingering.

When dusk built enough momentum, he began walking; sticking to shadows so no one would see him. He took the same route he used the day before. When he got to the deputy's place, he hid out back and waited for the man to get home. As far as looks went: he wasn't bad, not beautiful, but certainly not ugly. But he smelled! Not bathing for days built up stink, and a stinky woman didn't do well with men, well, not most men. The deputy was a dweeb, so Cil had a chance. A little after nine, the officer drove up. Cil waited for the man to get comfortable. After about an hour, Cil knocked on the front door, which was elevated with wooden stairs. He heard the recliner bend back. The deputy answered the door still wearing his uniform, sans shoes — the bullshit session began.

CHAPTER THIRTY-FIVE

The deputy was awfully trusting for a cop, but breasts did that. Cil was inside in no time. The story was she broke down on the highway while traveling to DC to visit her mom. She jumped across the highway rails and saw light from the golden arches of McDonalds, then saw the dirt road. She walked until she saw the police car, and here she was. He offered water, while Cil sat down on a chair by the kitchen table. He managed to spill a few tears, that sealed the deal.

"Let me get my shoes. We'll go check out your car." The deputy said.

He was nervous and fidgety; it was very rare he had a girl over. Thinking fast, Cil feigned exhaustion.

"Listen! I know this sounds strange, but can I just stay for a while. It's too dark to see what's wrong with my car — maybe we can do it tomorrow. I'll be out of your hair after sometime. I can sleep in the car, but I just need a minute."

Then something came out of the deputy's mouth that surprised him.

"You can sleep here tonight, if you want."

That was the response Cil wanted. He smiled and thanked

the man, who disappeared for a minute and came back with a blanket.

"Have you eaten, yet?"

"I haven't had anything since yesterday." Cil lied.

The deputy went to the kitchen and made some scrambled eggs and toast. He brought the plate out to the disheveled woman sitting on his couch. It looked and smelled good, so Cil ate without talking, that made her look more desperate. The deputy sat back down in his recliner; he was thinking of something to say. Cil finished the eggs and brought the plate to the kitchen, placing it in the sink. Next to the toaster was a knife set placed in a generic wooden case, the kind you get at Walmart. Cil reached for them but pulled back, *I gotta live in that body*. The guy was a cop - a nerd, but still a cop; sneaking up behind him was too risky since he was a she, the strength required to knock a man down just wasn't there.

"Can I use your bathroom?" Cil asked.

The deputy got up and pointed to where it was, then sat down. Cil went in and closed the door. He immediately searched the medicine cabinet on the wall, above the sink. In a little orange plastic receptacle, he saw a prescription for Ambien, a sleeping pill — did luck go his way? He emptied three pills onto his palm and crushed them using a shaving cream can. The deputy had a glass of what looked like iced tea next to him, on the recliner. The only thing Cil had to do was get the powder mixed with his iced tea. So far, it was easy going and the man was eager to please. Cil walked back out with his left hand closed, into a loose fist, and sat down on the couch.

"You have done so much already, but do you have any aspirin? My head is killing me — probably from the stress."

The deputy got up and went to the bathroom.

Shit! I hope he doesn't notice the missing pills.

The man came back with two aspirin and handed them to his guest. Cil barely made it back to the couch after mixing the powder into the iced tea. They had small talk while watching TV. The deputy was fond of reality programs and he loved watching "Survivor," a show where contestants are rewarded for their surviving skills in the wild while knocking each other out of the game. Cil had seen the show before, but not the current season — he was busy with other stuff. The show ended and the deputy put on another; he was two weeks behind, but wasn't awake for the dismissal at the end.

***

Time to get to work. Cil sat next to the recliner and did his incantations. The TV was loud, it played with his mind so he stopped and turned it off. The deputy was sleeping deeply. Cil resumed his position. After he incanted, there was the moment of transference — where space squeezed into a vacuum and everything became blurry. Then the reorientation phase, but since he gave too many pills, nothing happened. He didn't stand up and see the woman he once was. Inside his new mind, he swam around in a mess of lines and pictures, most not making sense to him. He pulled at his conscious until he managed to squeak open his eyes, but the blur remained. The woman was laying on the carpet, the TV was off, his arms felt like thousand pounds when he tried to lift them. He had to get to the woman before she woke up and freaked out. There was a struggle, of course, as two minds fought for dominance. Interestingly, as geeky as the deputy was, his mind was strong. Cil continued to fight until he defeated the other. He landed next to the woman. Groggily, he pulled off his belt and slowly wrapped it around the woman's neck, but lacked the strength to yank it hard. After three rest breaks, and in between the lure of the pills, he built up enough power to tighten the belt around her neck. He leaned back with the loose end of the belt until he felt she was gone. Then the deep got him, he faded into the black.

When he woke up, it was still dark outside, but the light wasn't far away. Getting up, he saw the body on the floor; he had done enough. He went to the kitchen sink and splashed cold water on his face — it helped a little. He had no idea if he had to work that day, but if he did, he had to be there at 9:00 a.m. On the wall next to the sink was a calendar, with notes written on dates. There was a dental appointment, dry cleaning schedule, and luckily, his work schedule, but he didn't know what day it was. He rummaged in his pockets, found a cell phone and looked at the date — it was Thursday the 25th. He checked the calendar and saw that it was his day off: *another break! But what about the body?* About a minute of thought, he muscled it into the bathroom and into the bathtub. It would be fine there for a while. From his observation, the deputy wasn't exactly a lady's man, so any scare of company coming over dimmed, as the light outside strengthened. As he walked out of the bathroom, the stink came to him. He remembered his short life in the woman's body and immediately knew where the smell came from.

Well, shit! might as well take care of it now. He knew that there was a small storage shed out back. Without changing clothes, he went out the back door of the trailer. The morning was coming, so he was quick. Inside the shed was an assorted mess of tools: a lawn mower, a weed eater, a bunch of spider webs, and what looked like a broken trampoline. He took a saw from the wall and went back inside. Entering the bathroom, the smell once again entered his nostrils; it brought him back to New York. He stripped himself naked and threw the bundle of his clothes into the bedroom, and went to work.

Cutting a body into pieces took time, more time than Cil thought it would. The saw was old and dull, but the bones were strong. He started with the head; he had experience with that, and went to work on the arms and legs — it took a long time. As the metal teeth of the saw met the flesh, muscle tissues ripped open and blood flowed freely, most of which went down the drain. The last thing he needed was the tub to stop up, so he plugged it and finished up. The torso was alone, with the other five parts littered about, yet the legs were too long, so he went back to work and cut them in half. Red spackled the cheesy tub tile and his arms were crimson. He turned on the water and washed himself off; the bright red diluted and the tub was full of human soup. He had to strain the mess and put the body parts into something so he could dispose of them. In the kitchen, he found a spaghetti strainer which he used to carefully pack the body parts into a suitcase, but he stopped with the torso, which he raped, rested and raped again.

CHAPTER THIRTY-SIX

It was morning, and he dressed for work. The body was in the suitcase and it was in the police cruiser's trunk; it was safe for a while. He would dispose of that thing after work. It was his first day as Cil Franklen, a deputy in a podunk town in America — he felt good. He drove his car to the station and walked in like he had been there for years, but didn't know where his desk was.

"What the hell are you doing boy?"

It was a yell from across the room.

Cil looked up and saw the sheriff standing in the doorway of his office; he filled it out.

"I'm getting ready for work, sir."

"Well! you might want to sit at your own desk, not at Sherril's."

"My desk?" Cil asked.

"Yea, your desk! Jesus boy! You've been here a week and you can't find your own desk? What did they teach you in Arizona?"

Deputy Albert Smith was from Tempe, Arizona. He got up and walked toward the desk the sheriff was pointing at. When he sat down, the big man shouted again.

"Don't get comfortable boy, we got a problem down at

the grocery store. Some punk kids drew a big penis on the window, probably the Riggins boys. Take care of that."

Cil got up and headed to his patrol car. He didn't know who the Riggins boys were, but it was time to earn his keep and play detective. With a town this small, it couldn't be that hard. As he drove to the grocery store, he looked at the town's people milling about and made a mental checklist for his first kill; the thought bent his brain. When he arrived at the store, the manager was pitching a fit and yelling about taxes, punks, and the lack of oversight by the police department. Cil listened and took it all in stride. When the pissed off man was done, Cil whipped out his notebook and jotted stuff down.

"Did you happen to see who did it?" Cil asked.

"It happened last night, but I've got the little bastards on camera. It was those fucking Riggins boys. I swear they are gonna wind up in prison, fucking little brats. Why don't you do something about them and their drug addicted parents?"

"I've only been here a week, sir. Give me time. I'll take care of it."

"You better. Bob is easy on those boys, on an account of their parents being losers, the elections are approaching, son. Do remember that!"

Bob was the sheriff — Bob Banacis, born in King's Crossing. He became sheriff twelve years ago. For a town of little crime, he did a good job, but he was biased on certain things since he was from this place. Kicking up loser parents wasn't that easy, plus they voted too. Cil took more notes and left, assuring the manager everything would be fine. When he got back in his car, he radioed the station and found out where the Riggins boys lived. When the secretary finished, the sheriff got on the radio.

"Listen, Al! Go easy on those boys. I'm sure you heard from Keever that they are messed up kids. Put the fear into them, but leave it at that. Got it?"

"If they did it, I was gonna bring them to the jail and let

them sit in there for a while. That will scare them."

"NO! Don't do that. I'm telling you boy, yell at them, yell at their parents, but you will not put them in jail. They need a father-like figure and I don't have time for that. It's now a part of your job description. Square them away and get back here. We got other stuff to do."

Cil grunted.

"Got it, sheriff. I'll be quick."

***

The weather was turning sour and dark clouds built up in the sky. A few rain drops hit the windshield and Cil temporarily forgot about killing. This deputy stuff was interesting; he was getting the hang of it. When he pulled up, he saw two teens running around the unfenced front yard shooting at each other with BB Guns. One of them took a shot at his car, that pissed him off — he got out with his weapon drawn.

"Put the gun down, you little shit." Cil yelled.

The kid laughed and ran into the house, followed by his older brother. Cil got out and ran to the front door, but went back to lock his car up — he knew what could happen with that. He knocked for five minutes, but nobody answered. He was about to kick the door, when a car pulled up and a scroungy couple got out. The man was roughly hundred and twenty pounds and the woman was about forty pounds less. They looked fucked up, and they weren't coming from the church. When they walked toward Cil, choice words escaped from their mouths which Cil could barely understand. In the mix of all the cussing and garbled stuff was anger, and the question of why Cil was there.

"Your kids sprayed graffiti all over the grocery store. I'm here to make sure they don't do it again."

More cussing and unintelligible stuff came out; Cil had enough.

"You know I'm a police officer, don't you? Are you two so fucked up you can't see that?"

Then the man dropped the sheriff's name, which made Cil madder.

"The sheriff isn't here, I am. I don't give a rat's ass who you know. You have been sticking your dirty titty in their mouths for too long, but your damn kids are gonna behave from now on. I may be new here, but I'm not gonna take any shit off from you two degenerates."

At that, the couple went into their house and locked the door. One of the kids, who shot at his car, peeked his head around the curtain of the main window and smiled. Cil winked at him and went back to his car; he had his next victim. The sheriff, the secretary, and the man who owned the plumbing store laughed when he arrived back at the station. On his drive over, the Riggin's boys' father made a call and swore up a storm about how the new man in town yelled at him and his wife in front of their kids. Bob didn't care much — his man did what he was told to, but it was funny.

"What else do you have for me?" Al asked.

"Nothing. I just wanted you back here so I could keep an eye on you. You're new and I don't know what you're capable of, yet. Get on with some of that paperwork on your desk and when something comes up, I'll let you know."

Cil sat in front of his desk and did the paperwork. That night, a few hours after he got off, he stalked out the area where the locals did their meth. He was hoping those Riggins boys would show up and they did. Quietly exiting his car, he stalked them in the darkness until only the brothers were left behind. When he was sure the coast was clear, he walked up to the boys and sat down on a cinder block.

"Well, what do you have in this pipe, boys?"

The younger brother looked like he was going to make a run. Cil drew his weapon and aimed it at the boy's head.

"I'll shoot you dead, you little shit. Where's your attitude now?"

"What the fuck do you want?" The older boy asked.

He still had his attitude, but his arrogance made him doubt Cil's intentions — Cil liked it.

"You're going to smoke all that shit right now. I mean, all of it! And I've got some more for you."

Earlier that day, Cil slipped into the evidence room, which was little more than a closet, and swiped a good size bag of meth.

"That's it? Shit, man! Ain't no problem with that."

He took a long drag on the pipe, exhaling a puffy cloud of chemical smoke into the damp night.

"Take another one." Cil ordered.

The older brother did and passed it on to his brother. It took about twenty minutes to extinguish their supply. Cil threw the bag he had on the dirt in front of them.

"Now smoke all of that."

"That's a lot of shit, man. We can't do all of that."

It was a big amount, enough for 4-to-5 grown men.

"You're going to, or I will take this knife and cut off a finger every five minutes until all that shit is gone."

"Fuck you!"

"You two are walking abortions. Here, let me motivate you."

Cil got up, kicked the younger boy to the ground, and cut off his pinky finger. Blood was thin, so it splattered everywhere; the boy howled in pain.

"Your turn!"

The older boy picked up the bag and loaded the pipe. The lighter lit up the space around them in the night. He drew in the chemicals deep and long. When he exhaled, the smoke drifted Cil's way; he liked the smell.

"Finish all of that in the pipe."

The boy did, then he passed the pipe and bag to his brother — the glass was refilled. The procedure duplicated and both boys were shaking. Again, and again, Cil made them fill the pipe and smoke until the entire bag was gone. They were chatterboxes by now, they laughed and talked so fast that Cil couldn't understand them. After a few minutes, both boys were on the dirt and fixated on the sky – the beautiful starry sky. It was a Monet painting with two meth heads disturbing the view. Cil looked at them without pity and suffocated them. The still night offered no help. He got back to his trailer — darkness covered it all.

CHAPTER THIRTY-SEVEN

"*KNOCK! KNOCK! KNOCK!* WAKE UP, BOY! WAKE UP! YO' AL!"

Cil sluggishly woke, thanks to the banging on the door. Sheriff Bob stormed in as soon as the door was opened.

"Your 'fear of God' shit didn't work so well, boy. I got two dead kids in my morgue and two fucked up parents filling up my station with water. Get your ass dressed, and come down to the station, ASAP!"

The sheriff looked around the trailer and shrugged.

"Clean this place up, it smells like death."

"What's going on?"

"The Riggins boys are dead, smoked their meth until they choked on their own air. I knew it was gonna happen sooner or later, but I figured their mom or pop would go first. Get down to the station, we got work to do."

Bob left the same way he came in.

Cil put on his uniform and drove slowly. He wanted the drama to ease a tad by the time he arrived at the station. When he got there, the parents evil eyed him as he walked through the open door.

"You did this." The mother said.

"Look in the mirror, baby. That's where you will find the one who did it," Cil said smiling.

The parents left after two hours. Cil accompanied Bob down to the morgue, where autopsies were being done. When they got to the cold room, Bob took out a little jar of Vicks and rubbed some under his nose, then handed it to Cil,

"You're gonna need this."

Cil did as he was told and they walked into the room. The coroner, Marmaduke Wilson, had finished with the young one and was getting started on the other.

"I don't have to tell you how they died, sheriff. You already know. I've dealt with this poison for too long. These boys consumed a larger quantity that sufficed to scramble their insides. Someone's bringing this shit into King's Crossing. We've got to find those bastards. Our little graveyard is running out of space."

He cut into the boy's chest and pulled out a lung.

"See this? This should belong to a fifty-year-old. Watch this."

He took his scalpel and sliced the lung, smoke drifted out.

"That ain't right."

They left, leaving the coroner with the dirty stuff. The drive back to the station was quiet. Cil planned on his next move — the parents. He mused at how he schemed right next to the sheriff, who didn't know anything — *right as rain*. The rest of the day was filled with paperwork, and Cil kept to himself. The deaths of the two kids left a mark on the town, only a little one. Most of the town's folk were actually happy about it, which was messed up in its own right. Such is life. When his shift ended, Cil headed home with anticipation; his body tingled with it. He couldn't wait to kill those two; he reasoned that the world would be a better place without them.

***

The trailer still stunk when he got back, but he put off cleaning. He changed into a pair of jeans and a flannel shirt that looked like rhubarb pie; it was ugly as hell, but warm. Cil liked the night, his bad dreams had taken a hiatus lately. He was thankful for that. He left his vehicle at home, turned on the TV with the volume loud, and slipped out the back door. He let the star lights guide him to the dilapidated home of the Riggins. The walk took a while but it was pleasant; it gave him a chance to clear his mind. The lights were on, so he cut a wide circle around the place looking for any life. Feeling safe, he moved closer and peaked in through the living room window. The mother and father were taking turns bringing out cooked products to the table. They had a good amount on their plates. White smoke filled the room and Cil's stomach rippled a bit. He decided on a direct approach and knocked on the door. Nobody answered, at first, but his persistence paid off. The door opened with the mother looking like an albino ghost. Cil punched the bitch as hard as he could. She fell back and he kicked her on the chin on his way to the room where the father was. The prick was surprised when Cil ran at him and punched him the same way. He was so messed up that the first hit barely fazed him. Cil kept hitting him until he had a blood bath. Cil brought a rope with him which he cut in half. It was an old house, and there was a sturdy beam going from the living room to the kitchen. Cil tied the ropes off there. He had to look online to find out how to make a noose. Although shabby, they would do the trick. The woman was first. Cil easily picked her up, and using a chair, he wrapped the rope around her neck, then let go. She grabbed the rope with her hands and she sucked in the air, but it was useless — she died quickly. The man was a little heavier but still skinny; it was no trouble at all. They both died the same way. When the man's neck was nicely wrapped, he picked him up and threw him. He heard the bones break. He died quickly as well. He watched the two hanging, but there was something he wondered about.

The woman was wearing sweat pants and a flower shirt. They would have looked fine on a pretty girl, but on her, not even close. He cut the shirt away — she wore no bra, as there was hardly anything to hold in. Not impressed, he pulled off the sweat pants. She was wearing sexy underwear – cheap sexy underwear. He pulled those down as well. She was shaved. Cil spread her legs apart and explored. He tasted her, but in an act of fervor, he used his knife and cut her down. He pulled down his pants and underwear, and ravished the dead body until he was exhausted. After a brief rest, he hoisted her back up and hanged her again.

He left.

***

The next day brought even more yelling from the sheriff, of course. Four people were dead in a 24-hour span. They were all buried in the same graveyard, with the town picking up the tab on the gravestones. Cil was quiet for a week, then killed three more. One was a male hunter, the other two were more druggies. The sheriff was losing his shit while Cil enjoyed it. He took a few days off and killed five in one day; they died in a house fire. It took two days for the fire inspector to find out that lighter fluid was the culprit. Eyebrows were being raised, but still, they had no idea

Sheriff Bob finally lost it. At first, he chalked up the deaths as strange, but now he was certain someone was taking out his town — one-by-one. Twenty-six people died in fifteen days and he didn't have a clue. Until one day, when Cil arrived at work on a sunny Wednesday morning, Bob was waiting.

"It's so strange, how people started dying when you showed up. What do you think about that, boy?"

Cil wasn't ready for that, he pulled out an Oscar performance with his response.

"I'm a cop! What? You think I killed all those folks? I know it's been rough, but this is ridiculous, sheriff."

Bob looked at him for a long while.

"It's just mighty peculiar that this crap started a little after you came here — after you took the job. I'm running out of straws here. First the boys, then their parents, then a lot of other people I know — we all know. You're fucking sitting there like the wind just blew a sweet tune up your ass. Give me some feedback, damnit."

"I haven't killed anyone — Jesus! Do you realize how dumb that would be? Shit Bob, most of the deaths were from drugs — look at the whole country, see how many die from that stuff. A hunter died from his own weapon and someone left their cigarette burning. People die, Bob! It's all explainable if you look at it. Run me if you want — you'll see that my record in Arizona is perfect."

"I already done that. Shit, I've emptied our coffers, dry running checks on people for the last two weeks. All right, I admit I'm losing and I am taking it out on you. This is pretty ridiculous, but I had to find out. My head is gonna explode soon and you might have to clean it all up."

Cil took a mental breath and stood up. He had caught a break with the coroner not finding out that he raped the mother of the two-trouble makers.

"Have you thought about a serial killer, Bob?" Cil asked.

"Yea, I have. I've thought about that a hundred times, but it doesn't fit. Here? How? Why?"

"We've had serial killers in Arizona, but I'm not a detective. I knew about them, of course, everyone did. You can't try to understand them, they just exist. Sometimes the wiring goes wrong, Sheriff. Sometimes they kill in their home town and sometimes they kill away, but if they want to kill, they will kill."

Cil's arrogance was shining through, like a beam of tainted sunlight; he pressed gently.

"Might have to bring the FBI in on this one, Bob."

"Yes, I know, but I don't want some government tool doing my job. I'm the damn sheriff. Fucking serial killer on my watch. This is gonna mess up my record."

"What about the victims?"

"Yea, them too."

Another day came and went like the writings of a dead poet. Bob called the FBI office in Minneapolis and gave the scoop. America birthed the monster, now it enabled information to travel quicker than before. Jacob Miller, who was still in Sioux Falls, South Dakota received this message pronto. He had been docile since Cil left, telling his boss his thumb was getting sore from being up his butt, but this news reinvigorated him. Sure, serial killers popped up every now and then, in all corners of the United States, but this one had a stink to it that matched the stink he wore. Within twenty minutes of getting the phone call, he was at a car rental place, and minutes later, he was on his way to King's Crossing. He left the chief of Sioux Falls without much information.

CHAPTER THIRTY-EIGHT

*T*wo hundred fucking miles! Miller pinched stuff together as fast as he could. If this was his guy, he was two hundred miles away, killing people like he was at Disney Land. *Why didn't he profile that? Shit, it was on the main highway leaving Sioux Falls!* He looked at his watch, it read 5:13 p.m., when he left, the chief's jaw dropped. It would take roughly three hours to get to King's Crossing. Even if he pushed 70, it would get him there by 8:30 p.m., or so. Perhaps it would be too late to do something that night, but he would be there. Cil knew where Miller was; he counted on him coming as fast as he could. He wanted to leave him a present for his arrival.

Cil drove through town looking for any riff-raff he could use. He had to be quick, as he only had few hours. He used his patrol car, got on the highway, and headed few miles east until he pulled over someone with a Cadillac. The car pulled over to the curb and Cil waited until he had a quiet slot. He walked up to the car. When the driver motored down the window, Cil reached in and cut the man's throat with a clean, strong pull. The man bled out and died with a surprised look on his face — he let it stay that way. When the seat was completely soaked with blood, Cil wrestled the man out and put him in his trunk. He left the Cadillac there with a white cloth hanging out of the window, which he rolled up. The glass was tinted, so seeing from the outside would be difficult. He locked it up and pulled away.

It was night, a police car on the side of the road was normal, although it slowed traffic down a bit. People always put on the red lights when they saw a cop — it was funny. When the coast was relatively clear, Cil took the body from the trunk and dragged it away eighty feet or so. He took a break, lit up a smoke, and watched the cars pass by; he went to work. At first, he cut off the head pretty clean, then he cut off all the limbs and laid them neatly next to each other. Close to where he was parked, a speed limit sign with a big 65, in black letters, illuminated when lights flashed on it. He grabbed some duct tape from his trunk and wrapped the head around the speed limit sign. Then, he did the same with the arms and legs, making a sick avatar of the former man. When he was done, it looked like a metal/flesh scarecrow. Lastly, he stuck a dollar bill into the man's mouth and pulled the car up so it would distract cars from seeing the sign for the time being. After an hour, he simply pulled away and went back home. He was bloody, so he took a shower and went to bed. Before the dreams took him, he imagined the FBI man's face when he saw his present and fell a sleep with a smile. *Have a Coke and a smile*, he giggled before he drifted.

Calls came in immediately. Sheriff Bob was at the sign when Miller approached the town. He saw the lights and pulled over. He was yelled at until he showed his badge, and hands were shaken briefly. Miller walked around the crime scene trying not to get in the investigator's way, but he had to see the body up close. This was a federal case as it spanned multiple states, but the Sheriff of King's Crossing and his people didn't know that, yet. Sheriff Bob didn't understand why the FBI man was there until Miller explained it, then it was almost a relief; it was out of his league, and he knew it. He yelled at everyone to let Miller do whatever he needed to do and stood by watching the profiler work.

Miller looked at the body. He dismissed the two guys looking for DNA and other stuff. After a few minutes, he went to his car, retrieved his camera, and took some pictures. It was a mess, but not as messy as it would have been had not Cil bled the body well. He walked around the poll, prodded with a pen, and looked some more. He called over one of the investigators.

"He wasn't killed here. There is not enough blood, but where?"

"Yea, I noticed that. I don't recognize him and I don't think he is from this town. You say you've been on this guy for some time now?"

"For some time." Miller said softly.

It embarrassed him that the man was still out there.

"He doesn't have an M.O. He just kills whenever he wants. This shit has happened in many states and I've been close, but that son of a bitch keeps slipping away."

He was tired of telling the story about reincarnation and kindly left that out, even with the sheriff. It would have to be told, but not right now.

"This man was brought here, so he would be missing from somewhere, unless he was driving through. Still, he is missing, but not legally. Well…"

Miller went to the sheriff.

"Have your men look for an abandoned car somewhere. It will be close. I think the victim was taken here — I know he was. If we find the car, we have a start. Then I have to explain a few things to you about this guy. Do you drink?"

"Do I drink? Shit man, I have permanent tabs at both the bars in town." The sheriff said.

"You're going need something strong for what I have to tell you, but first the car." Miller walked back to the body and lit a cigarette. In between the smoke and the people walking around, he pulled his thoughts together trying to figure out how it all fit. Eventually, the body was taken from the post and brought to the town's lab. The crime scene folks left, then the sheriff, Miller was the last. He looked around the highway and the surrounding land — *I'm here. Where are you?*

They all met back at the station. Bob called his deputy Albert Smith to the station. It was around midnight; the town was quiet — a beautiful quiet that reminded Jacob of a Norman Rockwell painting. Aside from the red and blue lights breaking the darkness, all was dark.

***

Cil heard the phone ring and knew. He dressed and headed to the station with an anticipation tingling his fingers. When he arrived, Jacob Miller met him with a handshake. Cil smiled broadly, but kept himself under control. The desire to spill was overwhelming. After coffee was made, the FBI man addressed the crew, starting somewhat slow, but finally building up to the beef; it wasn't digested well.

"Are you fucking kidding me?" Sheriff Bob asked.

He broke into a laugh and looked around to see if he was the only one. There were seven people at the station: him, Smith, his secretary, the two investigators, the coroner, and Miller.

"No, I'm not." Miller sighed.

Man, he was tired of explaining.

"I've done this speech before, and quite frankly, I'm damn tired of doing it. I've had a hell of a couple of weeks, so if you won't come aboard, get the fuck off. This guy is close and I'm going to get him."

Their mouths dropped; this was their first run-in with an FBI man and he was intense. They didn't want to cross him. Miller continued with his profile and left everyone with pupils dilated, except for Cil. He was paying close attention and Miller noticed.

"There is some information you need to know then." Cil broke the silence.

Sheriff Bob shot a stern look his way, but he continued.

"Twenty-six people have died here in the last couple of weeks, not including the one on the highway. That's a lot for a town this small. The sheriff thinks it is a serial killer, but I think it's just nature, and drugs."

The sheriff wasn't happy about that outburst and Miller saw that. There was some friction in the room, but the FBI man let it pass for now. He would talk to the sheriff later about it.

"Well, two and two makes four, and if that many people have died in your town, I think my man is here. He's most likely one of the town's folk and all of you know him, or her. This sounds like science fiction, and I know that well, but no matter how fucked up it looks like, it still is the truth. We have to deal with it and press forward. Put aside your beliefs for now and think about the impossible, because that is what's happening. This guy is changing bodies and killing people at will, and we can't catch him unless we open our minds to the improbable."

Miller paused for a second.

"I think it's best if we keep my presence here a secret — under wraps, for the time being. Let me blend in. This way I can see without prejudice. You have a small police force and we keep going as normal. He will slip up sooner or later."

"Yea, but if it's later, more people will die," Sheriff Bob said.

"People are going to die either way. It's not going to stop. Sheriff, can I talk to you in private please?"

Miller scooped up his folders and put them in his attaché case and waited for the staff to disperse. The deputy stared at him and it didn't go unnoticed. The few staff left the building, including Cil, who sat in his car for a few minutes, watching the front door to the station. When the two left in the building didn't come out, he went home wondering what they talked about.

CHAPTER THIRTY-NINE

"Sheriff, what's up with that deputy? He seems a little off to me."

"With all the shit you just told us, that is your first question?"

"You feel it too, don't you? Open the vault, Sheriff — fill me in."

Miller carefully looked at the man across the desk.

"He's new, from Arizona. My last deputy, Tom Forks, retired and headed off to Alaska; he was with me for sixteen years. I've got a friend on the force in Tempe. He recommended Albert, but I'm thinking I made a mistake. Wasn't long after he got here that the town started to thin, that was weird. I talked to him about it, but he just blew me off. I checked him out, many times, but he always comes up clean. I'm at a loss here man."

"Jacob Miller. My name is Jacob Miller."

"All right, Jacob Miller. I'm sure you've heard this before, but that's a big coincidence, and coincidences are only coincidences if something is ironic; nothing here is. It's pretty cut and dry — people started dying, and I'm fucking getting nowhere."

"That's an odd take, but ok! Let's keep an eye on him

anyway. Like I told you before, our guy, the Dollar Bill Killer, is somehow reincarnating himself and changing bodies. He's been doing it all across the country. I've got a death count higher than Bundy and Dahmer here — it's got to stop."

"Agreed! Where are you staying, Jacob Miller?"

"I haven't got that far, yet. I've been hoteling across the country so far; I guess that is what I'll be doing here, but I want to stay in the shadows, so to speak. The town's folk don't need to know that I'm here. It will be easier that way."

The sheriff shook his head.

"Why don't you stay with me. I have a spare room. It's small, but clean. You can remain as invisible as you want."

"I keep sporadic schedules. I don't think you would want someone crinkling papers at four in the morning. A hotel is just fine."

"Nope, the wife won't have that. The spare is on the far side of the house, so, I wouldn't hear a thing anyway, so you'll be fine. I'd rather deal with you than her. When you meet her, you will understand, Grab your stuff. Let's tackle this first thing in the morning."

Miller followed the sheriff the short drive to the house with his rental car. When they walked toward the door, Bob's wife met them, and gave Miller a firm handshake and lead him into the spare room. Any sense of intrusion he felt was extinguished with her smile. He laid down and tried to file the day's happenings, but his brain was worn out. Sleep quickly took over. It was a gentle much needed sleep. The sheriff and his wife turned in too. The lights went out, letting the night clean the day's dirt.

***

The sound of the pond, outside the sheriff's house, eased Miller out of his sleep into a rugged tranquil state. As opposite as they were, the two blended together to form a perfect sense of relaxation and alertness; something an FBI man needed to survive. Within minutes, he heard clanging in the kitchen and smelled bacon spitting grease into the fresh air. He slept in his clothes and they definitely needed a wash, but that was secondary. He smoothed his shirt as best as he could and smartly walked in to the kitchen, a cup of coffee waited for him.

"Did I wake you up?" Miller asked Bob's wife.

"No, I was afraid I woke you up. Here's some steal for you — it'll wax the sleep right out of ya."

She pointed to the coffee, which he sucked it down in two gulps. she refilled it.

"Bob will be right out. He has a morning ritual."

It was like an easy Sunday morning, and after eating breakfast, Miller was in a hurry to get to the station. Bob came out of the bathroom with a horrible comb over which he knew. "Don't you dare," was all he said. His wife went out to start the car, it was 6:43 a.m. The sun was just cresting over the horizon, oranging up the sky. Soon, the silence broke.

"Bob, you better come and see this."

Bob knew something was wrong when he heard her voice. Miller followed the sheriff out and saw the scared woman pointing at the front door; there was a dollar bill taped there.

"Mother fucker was at my house! He was here and I didn't know."

The sheriff's face wrinkled with fury as he reached for the bill, but Miller stopped him.

"Wait! Prints."

"What?"

"Don't touch it. There might be prints on it."

Miller turned to the woman and asked her to get a sandwich bag. She ran into the house and got what the man asked for. Miller took a pair of tweezers from his kit in his pocket, and gently peeled the tape from the door, and dropped the bill into the plastic bag.

"What kind of security system do you have here, sheriff?"

"Security system? This is a small town, son. Before all this shit happened, I didn't need a damn system. The town pretty much has an open-door policy, including my house. This ain't New York, boy. We're country folk, we usually take care of our own."

"Well, 'your own' are dying all over the place, sheriff. Anyway, we need to get this processed right away. This might be the break we need. We have that son of a bitch's prints now."

Miller put the bag in his pocket and made his way to his car.

"We'll take my car. You wanted to remain anonymous; this will keep you that way."

The sheriff and the FBI man arrived at the station; they were the only ones there. Calls were made, and soon the dollar bill was being scanned for the unique lines that made all humans identifiable. Both men stood in the quiet station. Bob called his deputy, at Miller's request, and told the man to take the day off. The sun warmed their part of planet Earth — Cil waited.

When a call came with the print results, both men were sleeping. The sheriff was in his office with his feet on his desk and Miller was in one of the jail cells, laid out on the thin mattress. Bob, startled by the ringing, kicked over the lamp as he picked up the phone.

"Yea?"

Only that one word.

"Sheriff, we've got the results. They belong to one Albert Smith of Tempe, Arizona, who I believe is your deputy. How did you allow him to tarnish the bill like that?"

Bob's head cleared pretty quick. He stood up, covered the receiver with his left hand, and yelled for Miller.

"Are you sure?"

"100%, sheriff. I'm faxing the results to you now, but I can come by if you want. Oh, there were other prints too, but they were smeared and old. Smith's prints were the newest."

"OK! Come on by with what you got; I'll be here."

Bob hung up, and met Miller in the station area.

"What's up?"

He was smoothing his pants with his hands, trying to erase the wrinkles.

"I fucked up, FBI man. Yea! I know you don't like that, but you were right. The prints came back and they belong to Al. What do we do now?"

Miller was fully awake by now. His right hand, almost as second nature, went to his weapon. A crooked smile developed.

"We kill the asshole."

"I figured you would say that."

CHAPTER FORTY

Does life explain the unnecessary, the weird, the odd, the fucked up and sick? Cil doubted it did, and while not really trying to find answers, he wanted to know. Little threads of conscious were woven in his brain somewhere, but they were old and dusty. They were the cheap threads, the kind you get in Korea or China, sewn into sleeves of cheap shirts and shoes; they were unseen. Why does it rain where it doesn't need to and not rain where is should? Why?

***

Cil pondered as he watched the sky, letting a quiet breeze run over his bloody body. The blood was dry and sticky, but it felt good — his second skin. He had just killed his last victim, but he didn't know that. It wasn't planned — the hurried nature of the kill led him close to imprisonment; he felt the doom of fucking up, but it had to be done.

Two hours ago, he was digging a hole. He thought he was far away from intrusion, but in a small town, far away wasn't far enough. He didn't hear the car and didn't see her until the flashlight beam sliced through the darkness. He climbed out, throwing the shovel a few feet away.

"Al, is that you?" The sheriff's wife asked.

The light went from his face, to the hole, to the wrapped body, and back to his face.

"Who is that?" He was trying to wave off the light like it was a cloud of flies.

"It's… Bob's wife. What are you doing? What's that all wrapped up?"

"A dog. I hit a dog on the road. I didn't want to leave it there."

But it was too big for a dog. He knew and so did she.

"A dog, huh?"

A brief silence.

"I know most of the dogs in town. Here, let me check its tag. Someone's gonna miss it. It wouldn't be right not to tell."

Sweat was running into his eyes and his temper slipped.

"It's a damn dog. Let me…"

He mumbled something, then regained his composure.

"I'm sorry! It just upset me."

He moved closer to the hole, but she would soon see the arm sticking out of the wrap — he had to do something. He stepped on the business end of the shovel and the handle sprung up. In one smooth motion, he grabbed it and swung it at the woman. The metal made a *clang* as it first hit the flashlight. He swung again at the woman's head; she fell immediately. He lunged down with the shovel again and again until blood splashed all over him. Out of breath, he dropped the shovel and laid down on the dirt. He knew this act complicated things — he panicked.

***

The sheriff and the FBI man were combing the town for Deputy Albert Smith, or whoever he was. It was just after 8:00 p.m. when they arrived at Smith's house. The GPS in the police cruiser said that was where the car was, but the place was empty. Jacob Miller had his gun drawn after Bob kicked in the door. The place was a mess, it smelled like death. Bob called his small forensic team and had the house checked. Blood was found on the living room carpet, bathtub, and kitchen sink. Any ambiguity and doubt ran out the window.

"If this guy has been busy as you say he has been, don't you think he's gotten pretty slick by now?" Bob said.

He and Miller were smoking outside.

"What do you mean?"

"Well, he's gotta be on to us, by now. I've already questioned him once. Even told him not to come the other day. He has to know."

Miller stamped out his cigarette on the dry wood of the deck.

"Of course he does. We have to get him now — today, before he slips town. Did he have another car?"

"Yea. We don't have the resources you city boys have, so calling in a copter ain't gonna happen. There is a lot of land out here."

"Let's get going. He's around."

The two men drove off after Bob gave orders to the men scouring the home. The sheriff's cell phone beeped; it was a voice message from his wife, but the message was hours old. He listened to his wife saying how she was going to get steak for dinner and wanted to know how Miller wanted his done. When he called her back, she didn't answer. He left a short message. He and Miller searched for another hour.

"If we're gonna be doing this all night, I gotta change my shirt: it reeks. Let's pop by my place, eat something, then we can resume. If he's around, we'll get him."

Miller didn't want to quit, but food sounded good. He needed it, so he agreed.

Bob's wife wasn't home when they arrived.

"Strange! She should be here by now. Let me find her

real quick."

Bob GPS'd her phone and got the area where she was.

"What the hell is she doing out there?"

"You have a GPS on your wife's phone?" Miller asked.

"Yeah! of course."

Bob answered like it was a stupid question.

"But you don't have a security system for your house?"

"Knowing where my wife is, and having someone dumb enough to break into my house are two different things, my friend."

"Where is she?"

"She's out east from here, a couple of miles, a little way from the pond. Can't figure out why though. I'll go and check. You can stay here and shower if you want. It won't be long."

Miller entertained the idea, but chucked it off.

"I'll come with you. You might come across Smith. I want to be there."

"Yup, figured that."

They both got back into the car. The GPS led them to a patch of land half a mile from the pond. They found the car with the keys still in the ignition and that disturbed the sheriff.

"Something ain't right, man. Let's…"

He was cut off by Miller.

"There's a light over there. It looks like a flashlight. Is she digging for gold?"

Bob didn't respond, he was running toward the light. Miller walked; he didn't want to get in the way of a domestic thing, but the yell changed that.

He ran.

***

When he got to where Bob was, the man was on his knees holding his wife's bloody head in his hands; it was crushed.

The sound of a vehicle being started creased the silence and the headlights disclosed its location, a few hundred yards away.

"Motherfucker!"

Bob screamed and ran to the vehicle, but it sped away, leaving dirt and dust to blanket the area.

"Bob, wait!"

Miller hollered, but Bob didn't stop. Eight shots were fired and none of them hit the target. Miller ran after him, but the truck was too far away.

"Is that Smith's truck?" Miller asked.

Bob ejected the empty clip and stuck in another one. He emptied that as well. Then he just fell to his knees.

"Come on. Give me the keys."

Bob didn't move for a second.

"Bob!"

"Sheriff!"

Bob's eyes looked up, but he was gone. Miller reached into the man's pocket and grabbed the keys. Bob took hold of Miller's hand hard, but quickly released.

"I'll drive."

CHAPTER FORTY-ONE

Miller steered the car while Bob loaded another clip into his gun, mumbling. It wasn't clear, but Jacob knew. They temporarily lost the truck, but Miller kept at him, following onto the main road going through town. He flipped on the lights and siren. One hundred feet behind, the sheriff leaned out the window and emptied his third clip into the darkness, hitting the tailgate of the truck twice. Cil quickly slipped down a frontage road, but Miller couldn't correct in time. He spun the car around and got back on track, but the truck was farther ahead.

"Give me your piece." Bob said.

"No."

"Give me your fucking gun, damnit! He's right there!"

Miller answered the same. He picked up speed.

"He's fucking leaving town. We can't do anything if he leaves town!"

Miller put more weight on the gas pedal, he crept right up on the truck's tail. Red lights came on and the truck slowed down, making the patrol car slam into the rear end.

"Goddamn, break check!"

Miller lost the engine, and he tried to start it again. The truck pulled ahead a bit, then rammed the patrol car. Now,

Miller pulled out his gun, but by the time he switched the weapon to his left hand, the truck sped off.

"Goddamn it! Go! Go! Go! Go!"

Miller turned the key. On the third time, the engine wheezed to life. The truck was a mile ahead. As they closed the distance, the truck cut a sharp left and headed to the old steam engine. Cil had a gun stashed there. He frantically tried to make to it before he was shot. There was no way in hell he had time to switch bodies, but if he could shoot the men behind him, maybe only wounding one of them, he had a chance. As he neared the abandoned train, he slipped the gear into neutral and drifted closely, jumping out when the vehicle coasted to a stop. He tripped on a pipe, got up, and ran into the train. He lifted the old couch to get to the gun, but it was gone. His mind warped into another speed of panic; he swore he left it there. The siren was close now, and Cil was out of time. He was sure he was done.

***

The light from the moon, almost full, trickled into the train through the window. He saw a fly sitting on a soda can. With no other choice, he began his incantations, speaking fast, but reciting everything solidly. Nearly a minute passed and the deed was done. The human body he, only seconds ago filled, slumped town and fell to the dirty floor. It took a while for him to adapt to the fly's vision; he was seeing everything multiple.

The sheriff and the FBI man entered the train.

His instinct, or that of the fly, was to jump up, turn to the left, and fly away, but he stifled that. His sight wasn't straight yet, and when the sheriff jumped on the body which was on the floor, the commotion knocked over the soda can. Cil took flight. Trying to focus his vision on the darkness outside the door, he lifted up and headed that way. He couldn't see it, but Bob was punching the confused man with everything he had. Miller stood over with his weapon trained on the poor guy's head.

"We got him." Miller said.

The sheriff slowly stood up and turned his gaze to Miller. His shoulders dropped. While Miller was reaching for his handcuffs, Bob grabbed the gun from him. The FBI man lunged, but it was too late. Bob fired three shots into the man's head. At that close range, the skull exploded.

Cil was almost at the door, but he couldn't see. Like flys do, he landed on Miller's neck. The instinct of the fly was strong and it threw up on the moist, salty skin. As he tried to force his will against the insect's, the man's right hand reached up and smacked the small furry thing. The fly fell to the floor. A slight pulse still remained. Cil tried to switch again — into Miller, but Miller's shoe put an end to it, then there was nothing.

Nothing at all.

OTHER HELLBOUND BOOKS

Stripper Noir

"I'm pretty much out of my "detective phase" now that I've finished Random, but I wanted to check it out. It's a nice detective murder thing with a twist and a very nice look at Vegas and the strip club scene. It's very accurate (as far as I know) strip club description and you never see that in a book, so that was nice. And a nice view of Vegas one doesn't usually get. I really enjoyed it." - Penn Jillette

Exotic Dancers are dying at an alarming rate in Las Vegas. Former LVPD detective, Frank Michi, is roped into helping not only his former partner, but also the New Jersey mobsters who run the strip club, to unmask the psychopath who is running amok killing the dancers.
Can he figure it out in time - before more girls are brutally murdered?

The Toilet Zone: Number Two
"Restroom reading at its most terrifying!"

Imagine, if you will, you're traveling through the unknown, hellbound, with no roadmap or stars to guide you. The light fades as you descend into a shadow realm where supernatural terrors make their lair and evil lurks at every turn. Here, dead things don't always stay dead, for this is a world where things that shouldn't be... *are*, and things that should be are not.

In this world, it takes between 2,500 and 4,000 reading words to pay a visit to the smallest, but terrifyingly necessary, room, and stories are written precisely to chill the bones as you wait for nature to make its call.

You open up the book, and one of the 32 tales skulking within its hellish pages chooses you...

It's too late to turn back now. You are about to set foot into another dimension, so best watch out for that signpost up ahead...You've just crossed over into... The Toilet Zone

The Erotic Odyssey of Colton Forshay!

Colton Forshay dreams himself into a bizarre sexual dystopia - a world in which nothing is as it should be, it alternately rains semen and menstrual blood, sickening sex acts and sexual violence are the norm, and the currency is deviant sexual acts.

In this dream world, Colton inexplicably finds he has gotten his dog pregnant and his wife is brutally murdered as a contestant on a popular TV show.

At first disturbed, then intrigued - and shamefully aroused - by his dreams of the other world, Colton is drawn in deeper and begins to spend more time there with the help of sleeping pills. His real-world wife forces Colton to see a psychiatrist, who encourages him to explore the dream world. And thus, our hero embarks on an odyssey with his dog/son, Eric, to discover the disturbing truth behind his dream world.

This is fantastical tale populated by a whole host of bizarre characters, set in an incredibly peculiar world. Chock-full of startling, sexy imagery and told with incredibly dark humor, Colton Forshay is a bizarro tale both engaging and disturbing.

Patrick Querney

The Horror Writer
"The most definitive guide into the trials and tribulations of being a horror writer since Stephen King's 'On Writing.'"

We have assembled some of the very best in the business from whom you can learn so much about the craft of horror writing: Bram Stoker Award© winners, bestselling authors, a President of the Horror Writers' Association, and myriad contemporary horror authors of distinction.

The Horror Writer covers how to connect with your market and carve out a sustainable niche in the independent horror genre, how to tackle the writer's ever-lurking nemesis of productivity, writing good horror stories with powerful, effective scenes, realistic, flowing dialogue and relatable characters without resorting to clichéd jump scares and well-worn gimmicks. Also covered is the delicate subject of handling rejection with good grace, and how to use those inevitable "not quite the right fit for us at this time" letters as an opportunity to hone your craft.

Plus... perceptive interviews to provide an intimate peek into the psyche of the horror author and the challenges they work through to bring their nefarious ideas to the page.

And, as if that – and so much more – was not enough, we have for your delectation Ramsey Campbell's beautifully insightful analysis of the tales of HP Lovecraft.

Featuring:

Ramsey Campbell, John Palisano, Chad Lutzke, Lisa Morton, Kenneth W. Cain, Kevin J. Kennedy, Monique Snyman, Scott Nicholson, Lucy A. Snyder, Richard Thomas, Gene O'Neill, Jess Landry, Luke Walker, Stephanie M. Wytovich, Marie O'Regan, Armand Rosamilia, Kevin Lucia, Ben Eads, Kelli Owen, Jasper Bark, and Bret McCormick.

And interviews with:

Steve Rasnic Tem, Stephen Graham Jones, David Owain Hughes, Tim Waggoner, and Mort Castle.

**A HellBound Books LLC
Publication**

www.hellboundbooks.com